HALLOWS WITCH

A SEASHELL COVE PARANORMAL COZY MYSTERY
BOOK 5

T. THORN COYLE

1

The sky outside the windows of The Widening Gyre grew dark, though it still felt early. I'd already busted out Rhiannon's heating pad and set it, turned on low, behind a stack of thrillers in the left side of the window. She had been curled up there, off and on, throughout the day, but was now wandering the shop somewhere. Perhaps visiting our newish residents, the gargoyles.

October on the Oregon Coast is no joke. As the days grow noticeably shorter, the wind whistles up the cliffs from the ocean, cutting through all but the most weather-ready coats. This isn't a cheery, apple-plucking, hay-wagon-riding time. It's a "get ready for the cold and rainy dark winter" time.

And I love it.

I think all witches love October. It is our season after all. Cauldrons and black cats and grinning jack o'lanterns everywhere. And the ending of the old year. A time to take stock and prepare for the year to come.

My father used to joke that witches got several chances at New Year's Eve. We have Samhain, the Celtic New Year, and then Yule, the winter celebrations, and the Gregorian Calendar New Year's Eve that we got to celebrate along with what Stefon's medieval reenactor crew called "the mundanes" and what I sometimes called "civilians."

This time of year, I missed both my parents fiercely. My mom died first, and my dad, much more recently. I'd inherited both my witchy nature and this bookshop from them.

They'd been appearing in my dreams lately, and I had the feeling they were doing more than saying hello. But whatever messages they were trying to convey were lost by morning.

No matter. Their messages would come through when the time was right.

I was adjusting a display of books on magic and witchcraft in the other side of the big windows from Rhiannon's bed, and sure enough, despite the warmth inside, I could feel some of the cold reflected in the glass. That signaled a harsh winter to come. I just hoped the bookshop's sales were robust enough to get us through til spring, when the tourists came back again.

At least Tracy and Tabitha, my two part-time teenage workers, had ensured a couple of more steady income streams through online book sales and the sales of branded Biff the Ghost T-shirts, notebooks, and mugs. They also wanted to start advertising the gargoyles, but I told them they'd have to talk with the living stone creatures about it first.

But for now, the shop was quiet. Just the occasional

sneeze from one of the gargoyles, who seemed to have caught a cold somewhere, and the soft cello music piping through the sound system set up by Biff himself, sometime in the mid-1990s, back when he was alive and owned the store.

The Widening Gyre was now mine. I'm Sarah Endora Braxton—yes, Mom and Dad also loved old *Bewitched* reruns, along with Stevie Nicks—and I'm a hereditary witch and town Justice. Luckily, I have a lot of help with both.

I looked forward to Samhain and the coming dark. Frankly, I could use a rest. Things had been hectic for months now. Sometimes the doldrums are nice.

I was using the time to catch up on the dreaded bookkeeping when the bells at front door chimed and in burst Tracy and Tabitha.

My best marketers tended to stop in after school, whether they were scheduled to work or not. They liked the place. Actually, the Widening Gyre is a lot of people's favorite place, a fact that made me feel good about continuing my father's legacy. I think it pleased Biff the ghost as well.

Tabitha was a skinny Goth with a dark blunt-cut bob and delicate Chinese American features framed by black eyeliner and dark lipstick. She reminded me a little bit of my ex-girlfriend and now best friend Cecilia, who was out of town at a classic car show. I missed her. It would've been nice to hang out while things were slow.

Tabitha wore black boots, black jeans, and a black anorak. Today she also sported a black sweater with a hot pink skull and crossbones grinning from the front.

Her partner in crime, Tracy, was a white, peaches-

and-cream blond-haired hereditary witch. Tracy wore a burgundy anorak over dark blue jeans and bright blue rain boots. Both teen's arms arms hung heavily with reusable tote bags, at least half of which had a stack of books and a cartoon ghost emblazoned on the side.

Like I said, the teens were master merchandisers. The tote bags were part of their handiwork, along with the T-shirt I wore under my own black cardigan. My shirt sported a stack of books topped by a black cat—Rhiannon—and surrounded by an arc spelling The Widening Gyre, Books and Gifts.

"What have you got there?" I asked.

"More Halloween decorations!" Tracy said, bouncing in her new Wellies. Tracy bounces a lot.

I stifled a groan and worked hard to not roll my eyes. It wasn't the teens, it was me.

Store decoration is my least favorite task, but the teens were right. The store did need more holiday atmosphere. I'd even been planning on getting to it, but just hadn't had the time. And really? I would've avoided the whole thing until it was too late.

"Show me what you've got." The teens plunked the tote bags down on the counter and began drawing out their loot.

"First, we have the scaaarrry spellbook," Tabitha said, opening up a heavy book with an embossed, fake-leather cover that looked like a creature was about to climb out. Sure enough, it glowed and cackled when opened.

"Well, that's pretty cool," I admitted.

"And you have...tiny witches' hats?" I drew out several stacked black paper cones with brims. They looked about the size to fit Rhiannon's head. "Are those for the cat?"

The teens snickered.

"What, do you think we want to risk getting our eyes clawed out?" Tabitha asked.

I looked at the front window. Still no Rhiannon, but I bet she'd be here in a minute. She always had an extra sense when people were talking about her, for good or for ill.

"We thought we could hang them from the ceiling of the front windows. So, they kind of hover over the books," Tracy said, face flushed with excitement.

"Hmm. What will you hang them with?"

"Clear filament. Fishing wire," she said, holding up one in each hand to demonstrate.

I had to admit that was a great idea.

"You know what? You don't need my approval. I trust you. You should just get to it. Are you going to do this today?"

"Yeah," Tracy said, digging black cardboard spiders from the bag. "My mom said she'd come pick us up and take us to dinner at the tamale parlor when we were through. She still has more work to do."

"Don't you two have homework?" I asked, suddenly suspicious. Both girls rolled their eyes at me.

"Study Hall," Tabitha said. "We both finished already."

The two were definitely too smart for school. And I knew that they were diligent, plus, if all of this meant I got more of their time in the store, I was all for it.

"Well, have at it!" I said, just as Rhiannon slinked back to the front of the shop, skirting past the laden bookshelves, heading for her heating pad.

"Rhiannon, Tracy and Tabitha brought little hats. You want one?" I waggled one between two fingers.

Rhiannon stopped and glared at me before popping up into the front window, settling into the warm spot.

"I'm warning you though, Rhiannon. I said these two are going to be invading your space pretty soon."

"Oh, that's okay," Tabitha said, "we can work on the other parts of the store first."

The front bells chimed again as the teens got busy and in walked Delta, all bundled up in a kelly-green raincoat, the type that are ubiquitous in the Pacific Northwest. She pulled back her hood, revealing her tousled gray hair and as she did so, out of her tote popped the purple peaked hat of Preston the gnome. Today's hat had waves embroidered around the edges. The gnome wore his own warm coat, and I knew that during the winter, Delta kept a blanket in there.

"Is your hat waterproof?" I asked Preston.

"It's wool," he replied.

Which I guess meant waterproof unless you were in a sustained deluge, which were exactly the kind of rainstorms we got out here on the coast. But maybe he was protected enough in the depths of Delta's tote bag.

And what do I know about gnome fashion anyway? Or any fashion for that matter? I'm definitely a jeans and T-shirt kind of full-figured witch. Luckily, my boyfriend, Stefon, likes me as I am.

I used to be Goth-inclined like Tabitha when my ex, Cecilia, and I went off to college in Portland, but being back on the coast had placed me firmly back in practical clothing territory. But my hiking boots were still black, and I usually wore black jeans.

Goth habits die hard.

"What brings you two in today?" I asked Delta, as the teens went about their decorating.

"I was thinking we should plan a community Samhain celebration."

Of course she was. All I wanted was a quiet night at home with a fire, and some time to figure out what my parents were trying to tell me.

But if Delta wanted a celebration?

That was probably what we were going to get.

2

Rhiannon peeked her black furry head up from the window display, looking interested.

"Community Samhain?" I asked. "You mean, like open to the general public?"

Witches were usually pretty private about our celebrations, and for a holiday dedicated to those who had passed beyond the veil? Well, that wasn't exactly for public consumption.

We had Halloween for that. Pumpkins, skeletons, candy, and fake ghouls, and all the rest.

Because, trust me, you did not want to encounter a real ghoul. Not that I have, but I've heard stories that make me shiver.

"What's this about community Samhain?" My Uncle Cyrus's smooth voice chimed in right before I heard the steps of his fancy, leather-soled shoes coming down the central aisle.

My bald, Black warlock of an honorary uncle was dressed sharply as always. Today's ensemble was black wool trousers and a black button shirt beneath a rust-colored Irish wool blazer. The only reason I know it was Irish wool is because he told me he got it on a jaunt to Dublin.

And by "jaunt to Dublin" I mean he had obnoxiously "popped in" just the way he had popped into The Widening Gyre. Yeah, I'm jealous that warlocks can bend space and time to their will like that. We witches must make do with bicycles, cars, airplanes, and boats to get around.

"Uncle Cyrus, are you ever going to text ahead as I asked you?"

He stepped toward me, arms open, and I walked around the counter and into his embrace. Frankincense and amber. My favorite smells, and since my parents had died, Uncle Cyrus's scent was the smell of home.

"Texting spoils the surprise." He released me and stepped back. "Hello, Delta. Preston."

Both witch and gnome nodded at him in greeting.

"Delta is the one who thinks we should have a community Samhain, so I'll let her explain."

Rhiannon made a daring leap from the front window onto the long counter, almost knocking over a pen display. Luckily, she didn't take down any of the decorations Tracy and Tabitha were busy with. Neither girl had said anything yet, but it was clear both the teens were listening intently.

::Spill it, witch.::

"Rhiannon, don't be rude." That's what I said out loud, but inside? My thoughts echoed the cat's.

Delta cleared her throat as Preston climbed from the tote bag and onto the counter, where he and Rhiannon went through some elaborate gnome–cat greeting sequence. I turned my attention on the gray-haired witch.

"More and more magical beings are moving to the area, and I thought it might be nice to have a Samhain tea, followed by a brief interfaith ritual."

"Interfaith ritual?" Tabitha said. "Ouch!"

Every head swiveled toward her. "Sorry. Stabbed myself with a safety pin. But what do you mean by inter-faith? Like, invite Muslims, Buddhists, Christians, and Wiccans?"

Delta shook her head. "No. I mean invite beings of a variety of magical stripes. Every group has its own rites and rituals and ways to honor the departed."

Huh. I'd never much thought of that, but supposed she was correct. Like, did the centaurs celebrate the season? Or the chaneques in the garden next to Vargas's Tamale Parlor?

Delta tapped a finger against her lips, clearly think-ing. "But we could invite the Wiccans too, I suppose. And perhaps any local hoodoo practitioners..."

"Your idea has merit, Delta," Uncle Cyrus interjected. "I will suggest it to the council and see if we wish to participate en masse, but I've a feeling many individuals will be keen to attend."

"Really? That snooty bunch?" Sometimes the truth bursts from my mouth before my brain catches up.

Cyrus glared at me but said nothing. I could hear Tracy and Tabitha whispering excitedly to each other and Rhiannon and Preston looked like they were in a staring contest, but I was sure they were discussing the proposal.

Thankfully, the bells on the front door shook and

chimed as Angie from the Blueberry Café burst through the door.

"Trouble!" she shouted. She'd clearly thrown an anorak over her usual uniform of Danskc clogs, jeans, sweater, and a blueberry-blue apron. The blueberry-blue kerchief that bound her short blond hair back off her face was askew, and her pale round cheeks were flushed with panic.

Angie was another full-figured woman like myself. Plus, she made the best muffins in town. Is it any wonder we were friends?

"What happened?" I asked, as Angie stood panting in the middle of the entryway.

"Someone left a huge dead rat on the café doorstep this afternoon, and a message in blood on the window."

"Seriously?" The word was out of my mouth before I could call it back.

"Of course, seriously!" Angie yelled. "Do you think I ran here for my health, when I should be heading home for a well-deserved bubble bath?"

My friend was fuming, and I couldn't blame her. She was clearly frightened. I would be too.

"Sorry, Angie. That was just reflex." I glanced at the clock. "It's dead in here. I may as well close."

Dead as a rat.

I scribbled a "closing early" sign for the door, just in case any stragglers showed up. By the time I was done, everyone else already had their jackets on, and both Rhiannon and Preston were ensconced in Delta's tote.

Okay then. I grabbed my own weatherproof burgundy parka, flicked off the lights, and locked the door.

"Right behind you, Angie. We'll figure this out."

At least I hoped we would.

But I couldn't help but wonder who in the world would leave a threat like this on an October afternoon. Wouldn't they have been seen?

3

When we got down to the Blueberry Café, Clarita, Angie's assistant, stood guard in front of the door, arms crossed over her chest and a worried look on her face. Clarita's skin and hair were brown, in contrast to Angie's super-pale, and she was shorter, but the women looked slightly alike in their matching Blueberry Café aprons and jeans.

"Are you sure we can't clean it up, Angie?" Clarita asked.

"Trust me, I want nothing more than that thing gone," Angie answered. "But I really wanted Sarah to look at it first. Thanks for guarding the place."

Clarita shuddered and stepped away from in front of the door, revealing the object on the front mat.

"Holy Mother," I said, "you weren't kidding."

"That thing is huge!" Tracy said.

Rhiannon hissed.

"Rhiannon! How did you get out here!"

She glared at me. ::*I'm tired of being left out of the excitement.*::

"You have hardly... Oh. Never mind." The cat was out of the shop and there was not going to be any getting her back in until she wanted to.

We all clustered around the dead rat. It was a massive gray thing, though it looked slightly deflated. And was that blood on its furry neck? I looked from the rat to the window, and sure enough scrawled on the glass of the large, friendly picture windows that looked from the cafe onto Main Street was the word BEWARE in capital letters. *Red* letters.

I leaned forward to sniff, but besides a slight copper tang, it didn't smell like anything much.

I clearly needed to watch more mystery shows to see how a person ascertained how to determine what exact substance something was. It didn't smell like red syrup, though, and heck if I was going to touch the stuff to gauge consistency.

I stepped back and Tabitha whipped out her phone and began snapping photos of the message from various angles. She also captured a few snaps of the rat on the doormat. It lay directly over the block letters spelling Welcome. Guess that rat wasn't welcome after all. And neither was whoever left it there.

When I looked back at Angie, Clarita had an arm around the baker, and tears rolled down her cheeks.

"Who would do such a thing?" Angie asked.

Clarita *tsked*.

"Sarah will get them, won't you, Sarah?" Clarita swung her big brown eyes my way. They were steely with determination, as if she could stare me into solving the crime.

I lifted both my hands and dropped them in the universal gesture of *Heck if I know, but I'll try.*

Both women frowned at me, and Delta nudged my ribs.

Right. Find some reassurance, Sarah.

"I'll do my best. Both Delta and I will get on it. And if we need to, we'll ask the council."

I looked around and realized Uncle Cyrus hadn't followed us to the café. That was strange. Where the heck had he gotten to?

"Meanwhile, we need to clean this up and do something about the rat."

"Are you just gonna throw it away?" Tabitha asked, nose wrinkling and brow furrowed in question. "Seems like there might be traces of something you could get off of it, right?"

I look to Delta, who shrugged, but Preston poked his head out of her tote bag and then swatted Rhiannon, who jumped and glared.

::Scan for magic.:: Rhiannon thought into my head.

Right. Of course. That's what I was here for. I was a witch and a Justice and could scan for magical traces. At least in theory. There was still so much about my job I was still uncertain of.

"Guess I'll try," I said. "Can you all look like you're just standing on the sidewalk having a conversation instead of staring at a crime scene?"

Everyone hopped to attention and clustered into small groups, chattering awkwardly and unconvincingly.

Luckily, the streets were quiet, and they conveniently blocked me as I crouched over the mat.

Rhiannon sauntered up next to me and sniffed the air in front of the door.

::Smells like magic.::

My nose was not as keen as my cat's, but there was something off about the rat. I mean, other than the fact that it was dead. It didn't seem too long dead, though.

"Fresh kill?" I asked.

::Fresh kill,:: Rhiannon agreed. Well, she would know. Not that she ever hunted much, preferring the ease of a filled bowl inside.

::I would hunt if you would let me outside more.::

By more, she meant at all. The only time Rhiannon got outside on her own was when she escaped.

"Not happening, cat." I took in a deep breath and found my center, connecting to the earth beneath me and the gray sky above. I fed that connection into the seat of my witch's power, then opened up all my psychic senses. Seeking.

I passed my left hand, palm down, around six inches above the rat's dead body. Nothing.

Rhiannon sneezed.

::You have to get closer.::

Even in mind speech, I could hear the dry sarcasm in her voice. I shot her look.

Which she ignored.

"I don't see you touching the thing," I muttered, but lowered my hand until it hovered two inches away from the rat.

"Bingo." There was something there. A magical trace. I could taste it on the back of my tongue, which was kind of gross, let me tell you. It tasted of dirt, microwaved fish, ectoplasm, and roses. That was the only way to describe it, and I had no idea what would have caused that combination of magical signatures. I sent what I sensed to Rhiannon, who hacked as if she was about to cough up a hairball.

::That is disgusting. Tastes like a grave.::

"Oh!" I rose to my feet, stomach lurching from the magical traces—Rhiannon was right, they were disgusting—and worry.

"Oh?" Tracy asked, turning. Guess I'd said that out loud.

I looked around at my little hodgepodge crew.

"I think we're in big trouble. It's getting on towards Halloween."

"And?" Delta said.

"And I think we're dealing with a ghoul."

Delta groaned. "Then that will be ghouls, plural."

"Why plural?" Tabitha asked.

Both Delta and I answered at the same time.

"Because ghouls never travel alone."

It was clear we needed to do more research, but first, we had to deal with the mess.

"Could you?" Angie stood in front of me, holding out a pair of ancient blue dishwashing gloves and a several sheets of foil from the café kitchen.

Ugh. I nodded and was thankful when Tracy stepped forward to help. Together, we wrapped up the rat in layers of foil and stuffed the whole thing into a paper bakery bag.

Which I was left holding, of course. I grimaced but didn't complain. After all, I was Justice in Seashell Cove, and it appeared that dead rats were now part of the job description.

Not that this was a job I'd signed up for mind you, but it was the job I had.

Clarita and Angie were busily scrubbing the blood off the front window with Tabitha's help. They hadn't heard the conversation, which was good, because I needed more time to think before sharing what might only be a hunch.

"You need any more help here?" I asked. Clarita shook her head.

"We can take care of the rest. You go, Tabitha." Clarita looked at her boss who was scrubbing at the glass, trying not to cry. "And then I'll take care of her."

Clarita gave me a knowing look, which told me that she would brook no protests from Angie and would escort the bakery owner safely home and probably not leave until she was tucked up in her favorite pajamas with a cup of something warm and soothing.

I could use something like that myself, I thought, looking down at the bag in my hand.

But first, I had to figure out what to do with this rat.

And who was targeting my friend.

4

Leaving Angie in Clarita's care, we made our way back to my place, including Rhiannon, who decided she wanted in on the entire investigation instead of heading back to her cozy spot in the bookshop.

Carol said she would meet the teens there and fetch them dinner after our meeting.

A fire was laid in the hearth already—yay, past me— so all that took was the strike of a match. We were soon ensconced in my cozy living room, sitting on the sofa and overstuffed chairs around a crackling fire. Each of us held a hand-thrown mug with a nice cup of licorice-mint tea.

The rat was ensconced in an old metal trash can on my tiny back porch. I'd secured the top with a few old bricks, hoping that would be enough to keep other animals away.

I sure as heck wasn't having that thing rotting in my house, wrapped in foil or not.

"So, tell us about ghouls," Tracy said. Both teens had

their phones out, ready to type in whatever information Delta and I could give them.

I sipped my tea and thought a moment, scraping through what I'd gleaned over the years from my witch studies.

Rhiannon was perched on the arm of the sofa next to me, looking watchful, but offering no information. Delta didn't speak either. Must be up to me.

"Well, ghouls tend to haunt graveyards."

"So, they're ghosts?" Tracy asked.

"Not ghosts, exactly," I replied.

"They're not a type of vampire, are they?" Tabitha asked, leaning forward, voice urgent, "because if they are, I could ask my parents. If you want."

"No, they aren't a type of vampire," Delta chimed in.

"But asking your parents is a great idea," I said quickly. For one thing, vampires might actually know about ghouls, and for another thing, I had yet to meet Tabitha's parents and felt it was about time.

Tabitha sat back on the couch. "I'll ask them, but you know, they're pretty private."

I nodded sympathetically. It must be hard, having vampire parents and being surrounded by magical beings when you had no magic of your own. Tabitha was a Wiccan and had the magic any human could develop if they took the time. But hereditary magic? She hadn't a lick, but she made up for it by working hard with what she did have and held a lot of promise.

It made me wonder though, which came first, being Goth, or your parents turning vampire?

"Back to ghouls," Tracy interjected.

Right. Back to ghouls.

"Ghouls haunt graves. Some people think they're revenants, but most people just think they're a type of monster. Some legends say they can shapeshift, others say they consume the blood of children. Still others say they are carrion eaters, robbing graves and feasting on corpses."

"Really? Eww!" Both teens looked horrified.

::And people think cats killing small animals is disgusting. Hmph.:: Rhiannon settled into a more comfortable crouch on the sofa arm, black tail tucked around her, looking smug.

"Yeah. Pretty gross, though if you think about it, not so different from other carrion eaters. You can think of ghouls as creatures really into recycling and composting. You know, making use of what is dead so they can keep living, the same way crows, coyotes, or worms take care of..."

Tabitha and Tracy stared at me, mouths open in horror and disgust. Delta just rolled her eyes.

I sat back, slightly deflated. I'd been warming to the idea of ghouls being useful parts of the ecosystem.

"Okay. Maybe that's a bit much, but I'm not sure how much truth there is in the stories, anyway, and how much the tales arose to frighten people, children in particular."

"Frighten them why?" Tabitha asked.

She was always astute with her questions, a quality I'd come to respect. Even if she didn't like my ghouls-as-innocent-carrion-eaters theory.

"A lot of creatures who live on the dark side, so to speak, want their privacy, or are shy, or any number of things. It's natural that they would seed stories to keep people away from their, er, haunts."

Tabitha nodded, probably thinking of her parents.

"Or they're engaged in nefarious and evil practices that they don't want people to see," Delta said, calmly drinking her tea as if she'd just commented on the weather.

"I supposed that could be true, too. We need to consider this case from all angles," I said, sipping at my own cooling tea. I had to keep an open mind.

"We need to look at that rat again," Tabitha said.

I sighed. She was right. We hadn't really examined the thing properly, because, one, we'd been on a public sidewalk and two, eww. Guess I had to buck up and give my squeamishness the boot. I wished Stefon was here, but he had a big project due tomorrow and I wouldn't interrupt his work.

But having a big strong knight to look at a dead rat sounded a lot better than looking at one myself.

"Okay," I said, pushing myself up from the sofa. Let's get this over with."

We all trooped through the kitchen and out to the back porch. I grabbed some rubber gloves from beneath the sink, and some barbecue tongs. I wanted as much between me and the rat as possible.

"Ready?" Tracy asked, her blond hair gleaming in the porch light. She looked equal parts disgusted, worried, and excited. Ah, teenagers. Everything was a new experience to them, and they hadn't yet learned to run far away from the unknown.

Not that edging close to thirty kept me out of trouble.

Using the tongs, I lifted the layers of plastic bags from the can and set the bundle on the porch.

Tabitha handed me the gloves. Great. Guess I was the one unwrapping this particularly unsavory present.

The plastic crinkled. The dead body lurched. I jumped, then forced myself to calm the heck down.

It was just a dead rat. I'd already examined it once. And it couldn't hurt me.

Right?

Finally, I got the thing unwrapped and backed off enough for the others to see.

There we were, a circle of three hereditary witches, a Wiccan, a gnome, and a cat.

The rat looked a little bit like a deflated balloon. Its once dark and glossy eyes were covered with a gray film and stared at nothing.

"Who's going to test it?" Tracy asked, voice tentative.

"Test it?" Tabitha asked.

"See what kind of magic is at work," Delta replied.

Rhiannon walked over, stiff-legged, and sniffed the air above the rat.

::*There's the ghoul smell. And definitely some magic,*:: she replied. ::*But I don't recognize it.*::

"Delta? You want to give it a go?" I asked. I still wore the rubber dish gloves and wasn't planning on taking them off until I absolutely needed to.

Delta considered the rat. Preston considered the rat.

From a distance, the ocean pounded the shore. The sound was soothing, and the briny scent covered whatever decay was happening at my feet.

The rat really didn't stink much in the first place, maybe because it was drained.

"Give me space," Delta finally said. The teens and I all backed off. Even Rhiannon took a few steps away.

Delta crouched, knees popping, groaning slightly at the effort.

"Do you want a cushion?" Tracy asked.

She was always so helpful. Must have more than a trace of empath in her, which I should talk with Uncle Cyrus about. We were supposed to be training her, but anything official kept getting put off by various magical crises, so her training had been spotty so far.

Delta waved a hand impatiently, as if shooing away a gnat. I felt the change in the older witch as she went through the protocol all magic workers use to center themselves, open their senses, and get ready to pay attention to energy patterns just outside normal human awareness.

My own breathing slowed in response. I couldn't help it. For witches, it's an automatic thing: one person enters a state of centering and pretty much everyone starts to adjust in response.

Finally, she held her left hand over the rat, passing through the air above the poor, deflated creature, moving back and forth in even sweeps.

The rest of us waited in silence. A couple of cars drove by on the street out front. The ocean continued its slow crashing on the beach several blocks away.

I wondered about us all. About the coming holiday. The party Delta wanted us to plan. About being a witch, here, now, in Seashell Cove. About what my future might hold, once I was done examining dead rats....

"Rhiannon is right. This was definitely drained by a ghoul," Delta said, breaking through my reverie. "And there's a hint of some other magic around the thing—

maybe fae?—but there's another energetic signature, too."

"A third kind of magic?" Tabitha asked.

Delta wrenched her eyes from the rat, and dropped her hand.

"No," she said. "The third energy signature isn't magic exactly. This third strand is human. And it feels very disturbed."

5

The next day, I stopped by Angie's before heading to the bookshop, for my favorite combo of English Breakfast tea and blueberry muffin. It's not the healthiest breakfast, but it was the one I wanted.

And after examining a dead rat last night, it was the breakfast I felt I deserved.

I pushed open the door to the Blueberry Café, skirting past the jam-packed community bulletin board that bristled with flyers and business cards.

This was my favorite time at Angie's. It was the lull between the pre-work breakfast rush and lunch. There were a few folks with laptops open using the café as their office and what looked like two parents with their children in strollers next to the table at the front window favored by Delta Crabbit and Preston when they were around.

Clarita gave me a wave as I got in line behind a distinguished-looking man ahead of me. He was dressed far too well for Seashell Cove, in a black wool coat and nice shoes. Pale, silvery hair fell softly to his shoulders.

He reminded me a bit of Uncle Cyrus. They had similar taste. Angie, looking not her best, rang the man up without her usual smile.

The man turned and greeted me with a nod. His eyes were green, and there was something ethereal about him.

Hmm. Fae blood, perhaps? Before I could probe, Angie handed the man a white paper bag and he was past me in a swirl of that long, dark coat. Mysterious.

I took the man's place at the counter. Angie's face looked troubled, and her usually neat blue bandana was askew.

"Sarah," she said by way of greeting. "The usual?"

"Yes, please. And do you have a moment to sit? I have something I need to talk to you about."

That made her look even more worried, but she simply pressed her lips together, nodded, and rang me up.

I made my way to the back corner of the café, away from the big picture windows, toward the spot Angie liked to call the library. The space held a couple of tables and several comfy chairs with side tables next to them and was enclosed by two walls of books.

I sat down in one of the comfy chairs with a sigh and pondered what we had discovered the night before.

Who was the human or humans working with the ghouls, and why?

Soon enough, Angie was there holding a tray with a warm blueberry muffin, a pat of butter on the side, my tea with all its accoutrements and what looked like the largest cup of coffee the café sold. She sat the tray down on a side table and plopped into a second comfy chair.

"I don't get it. Who would do this to me?" she asked.

I shook my head. "I have no idea. Everyone loves you and the café."

"Right," she said, gesturing around the space. "What's not to like?"

I gave her some time to brood by splitting open and buttering the delectable muffin and took a bite of heaven.

"Angie, I swear I don't know how it's possible, but your muffins get better every day."

"Well," she said, "for one thing, I'm back to baking them now that Buster is gone."

Buster was a former employee who had turned out to be running a fairy dust ring that supplied the intoxicant to the local party contingent.

"It's hard to find good help these days. Isn't it?" I said, keeping my face straight. She looked at me, eyes big and startled, then caught the not-quite-a-joke and started laughing.

I laughed, too. It felt good.

She took a sip of coffee. "All right, spill. Why are you here?"

"Well, I have some pretty unpleasant news."

"Less pleasant than a dead rat and a scrolled message on my windows?"

"Well, see, we examined the rat last night...."

She sat down her mug and raised an eyebrow. "And?"

"It had been drained of blood."

"Like"—she leaned forward and whispered—"vampires?"

I shook my head.

"At least, I hope not," I said, thinking of Tabitha's parents. We were definitely going to have to enlist their help in this case. "We're thinking it's a ghoul."

"A ghoul? What's a ghoul?"

I poured some oat milk into my cup, then picked up the teapot, pouring out the fragrant golden-brown tea. Giving it all a stir, I leaned back to take a sip. I thought about how to explain.

"Ghouls are revenant types. They hang out in cemeteries. Drain blood. Scare children. You know, ghouls."

"This isn't just some Halloween prank?" She sat back heavily and groaned, scrubbing her hands over her face. "Okay. Ghouls," she said, picking up her giant coffee mug again. "But that still doesn't explain why the rat and the warning."

We sat in silence for a moment, Angie taking thoughtful sips of coffee, and me, stuffing delicious, buttery muffin into my mouth.

I chewed. Swallowed. Thought.

"Did anyone you know die recently?" I finally asked.

She gave me a sharp look. "No. And even if they had, what does that have to do with anything?"

I shrugged, wiped my hands on a paper napkin, and picked up my own mug. The tea was perfect.

"I'm not really sure," I said. "I'm at that place in the process where I'm grasping at straws. We need more information, but I'm not yet sure how to get it."

"Can you ask the ghosts?"

"Hmm. Of course. Why didn't I think of that?"

Now it was Angie's turn to shake her head.

"I don't know. Sometimes you magic people seem to

miss the most obvious clues that are right in front of your face."

"Right," I said, "like asking ghosts about creatures that haunt cemeteries. It's as good an idea as any, but we still have to figure out why they're targeting you."

"And why," she insisted.

That was indeed the million-dollar question, and one I had no idea how to answer. We were quiet for a moment, then Angie stood.

"Well, I have to get back to work. Text me if you find anything."

She left me to the remains of my muffin and my pot of tea. I needed to get to work, too.

Maybe the day's tasks would give my brain the rest it needed, and the answer would just appear.

Like magic.

It happened that way, sometimes, but unfortunately, I couldn't count on it.

What I could count on was that I had time to finish this delicious tea and scoot my butt to the bookshop.

I sipped and gazed across the shop toward the windows framing Main Street. It looked like such an ordinary October day.

But nothing in Seashell Cove is truly ordinary, is it?

6

After leaving Angie's, I knew just what I had to do. Checking in with ghosts at The Historic Kelpie Inn was a good idea. But first, I needed to visit the local cemetery. I still had half an hour before I needed to open the store. Might as well get some sleuthing in.

You might be thinking that going alone to a cemetery when there are possible ghouls on the loose was probably a bad idea. And I would agree, except it was broad daylight. Now granted, it was a gloomy October morning, but still I figured I should be safe.

Even so, as a precaution, I texted Stefon to let him know where I'd be, and sent out a thought to Uncle Cyrus, who still hadn't reappeared. I assumed that meant he was checking in with the council, but all I could do was hope that was the case and that he wasn't in danger somewhere.

Cyrus is a well-trained warlock and can usually take pretty good care of himself. And he has a warlock girlfriend who can kick some serious magical butt. But neither truth stopped him from getting captured before. One thing I had had to learn as an adult witch was that caution was called for more than I sometimes like. Caution goes against my nature, but I'm doing my best.

I walked back to the bookshop parking lot where I'd left my car, a used hybrid Ford that Stefon was helping me finance. I felt weird about that at first, but then Stefon convinced me to accept his help. "I love you, babe," he had said. And besides, he makes four times what I do. The car was a cross between an SUV and a car, and not nearly as cute and sporty as my little orange electric Fiat, though I have to admit that the bright turquoise beast fits my size-sixteen frame a lot better.

Settled in the comfy driver's seat, I put on some Stevie Nicks, pulled onto Main Street, then turned left, driving away from the coast into the hills above Seashell Cove. There were hiking trails and even a waterfall up here, places I didn't get to nearly often enough, preferring to go jogging on the beach with Stefon.

I wasn't headed to the main, larger cemetery, which was two towns away. Instead, I figured I should check out the tiny old plot that few people even remembered was here anymore.

Winding my way through the houses with the best views in town, houses I as a bookseller would never be able to afford, I turned a corner and gasped with delight. A giant old Sitka spruce sat smack dab in the center of the small cemetery plot. It was magnificent, though I wondered if it missed the spruce friends that must have surrounded it hundreds of years before.

The old cemetery was very picturesque, if not a bit creepy, with falling-over headstones, obelisks, and angels whose carved faces had softened with time. The place looked pretty well maintained, which made me wonder if Seashell Cove didn't pay Mr. Vargas for upkeep.

There were nicely trimmed hedges, and the grass between the headstones looked as if someone had taken a weed whacker to it not so long ago. As a bonus, the far edge of the cemetery had killer views of the ocean far below. Looked like the dead had the best spot in the whole town.

I parked along the sidewalk at the edge of the cemetery. The place was too old to have a parking lot of its own, and I bet it rarely got visitors, which gave me a pang of conscience and sadness.

I should probably come up here and leave some flowers or other offerings for the long-forgotten dead. Maybe that could be part of Delta's Samhain celebration. I'd have to ask her.

As I picked my way through the headstones, boots squelching in the grass, I paused to read some of the gravestones. Father. Mother. Beloved child. Treasured Aunt.

I looked around, not sure exactly what I was looking for. The place felt peaceful to me, not haunted at all. Whatever ghosts used to linger beneath the shelter of the spruce must have given up long ago. Considering some of the headstones were from the late 1800s and early 19th century, I was probably right. White people began settling in the area in the middle 1800s, displacing the Siletz peoples. That fight continued well into the late twentieth century. I bet the spruce had seen some things in its time.

I stopped next to the towering tree and placed a hand against the brown-gray scales of its bark.

"What do you think? Any ghouls here?"

"Ghouls? What do you want with ghouls, girl?"

The voice that answered me was decidedly not coming from the tree. I peered around the massive trunk and spied Serafina, the black centaur who seemed to be the leader of the local herd. Or clan. Or...whatever a grouping of centaurs was called.

"What is the collective noun for centaurs?" My brain blurted before my mouth could stop the words.

Serafina shook her head. "An eminence."

An eminence. Of course, it was. Centaurs weren't the humblest of creatures, were they?

"Why ghouls?" The centaur's mouth turned down into a frown, and she crossed her arms over her chest, covering her small, ahem, breasts. Which made me think. I'd never seen any busty centaurs. I would imagine galloping without a sports bra would have been inconvenient at best and painful at worst.

"Sarah!" Serafina's voice cracked through the cemetery, snapping me to attention.

"Sorry," I replied. "Something about this place makes my brain even more wander-y than usual."

Serafina pawed at the grass in irritation.

"Someone left a drained rat on Angie's doorstep, and we suspect it might be ghouls."

The centaur looked off toward the slice of ocean view at the edge of the cemetery, eyes thoughtful.

"I have seen a couple of ghouls around, but they're pretty harmless."

"Harmless?"

Serafina shrugged. "Not much around here to prey on, is there? There aren't a lot of families coming to visit this place. Mostly it's deserted. It's why we come here sometimes, just to enjoy the view. It's peaceful here. And besides, our people have a long-standing relationship with friend spruce here."

She jutted her chin toward the tree.

The centaurs mostly lived in the forests outside of town, only venturing in when they needed to. Or at least, that's what I thought. Clearly, they visited more often than I knew.

"So, what do the ghouls, er, eat then? How do they survive?"

"Rats. Squirrels. Birds. Other small animals. They don't need much. Just a little blood and some life force and they're good to go."

"Huh. So, they don't need to attack humans? Terrify children? All the rest?"

Serafina shrugged. "Some revenants do, I suppose. And there are bad people of all kinds. But like most of us, ghouls are just trying to get along."

"Live their undead lives."

"Exactly."

Did I mention that centaurs don't have much of a sense of humor? Stefon would say they were Vulcan-like in that regard. Except I'd seen Serafina's temper and watched another centaur cry. So clearly their emotions weren't broken.

Gah! There I went again, off on a tangent. Was I worse than usual? Was there something about this place?

I sniffed the air, and opened my other senses, trying to catch a whiff of magic.

Nothing. Just green grass, the smell of ocean, and a slight hint of the grave that must be the ghouls.

"Ghouls only come out after dark, don't they?"

The centaur looked at me as if I was a fool.

"Of course, ghouls only come out after dark. They're ghouls."

Then how did the rat get on Angie's doorstep on an October afternoon?

7

I pulled into the tiny parking lot on the side of the bookshop. Duncan was outside, arms crossed, shaking his head. I beeped the car shut and hurried toward him.

"What's the matter?" I asked, heart sinking when I saw the grim look on his face. He gestured to the door and sure enough, on the mat was another dead rat, and on the window panel of the door were the beginnings of a word, with a B, E W, and then trailing off as if whoever had been writing it had been interrupted.

"Oh no," I said. "You're kidding me. I was just here forty minutes ago, when I picked up my car!"

"Why would someone do this?" Duncan asked, running a hand through the shock of bleached-blond hair that graced the top his cherubic face.

Well, if cherubs wore heavy, black-framed glasses, and 1950s striped sweaters over old punk T-shirts and jeans.

"We're trying to figure that out," I said, staring at the

bloodred series of letters as if they were a code I could crack.

"What do you mean?" he asked. Duncan tends to tune out on his days off, focusing on creative projects and the like. So it wasn't surprising he hadn't heard.

"Someone did the same thing at Angie's yesterday afternoon. We thought it was ghouls, but..."

"Ghouls?"

"Ghouls. Like revenants."

"Like, things that haunt graveyards? Want your brains?"

"That would be movie zombies, but close enough." This was not the time to get into the differences between actual zombies and movie zombies. Pop culture, man. For everything it gets right about the supernatural, there are five things it gets wrong.

"Don't those kind of creatures only come out at night?

"That's the problem," I said. "They do. But they also drain small animals in order to survive. So, the drained rats make sense. But not the daytime deliveries."

"So, someone's trying to warn you and Angie about what, exactly? Like, are they threatening you? Or trying to ask you to pay attention to something?"

I sighed. The rat stared up at me with one beady, dead eye. I was going to have to hose down the door mat. Or replace it.

"I have no idea," I said, "but let's get this thing cleaned up."

Duncan wrinkled his nose in disgust. "What should I do with it? Just throw it in the compost bin?"

"No," I said, "we'd better wrap it up. I should take it home with the other rat, just in case."

"Are you sure about that?" Duncan asked. He was right to be skeptical; I was skeptical myself.

"It's evidence," I said. "I would hate to put these rats in the compost only to discover they're carrying some important clues."

We both stared at the poor, dead thing, neither of us wanting to touch it.

Finally, Duncan got the store keys from his pocket, stepped over the rat, and opened the door with a clang of bells.

"I'll go get some plastic bags from the break room."

"And I'll start cleaning off the window," I said, "but I guess I'd better take some pictures first."

After snapping a few shots with my phone, I followed Duncan back to the kitchenette for cleaning supplies while he rustled up a few plastic bags.

We got to work out front. Luckily, the blood or whatever it was came off the window easily. By the time Duncan had the rat well wrapped up, the window was sparkling clean.

The shop windows should be washed more often. I should probably hire someone to do it at least once a month, during the summer months at least. Cleaning windows during Oregon Coast winters were useless, what with all the rain.

Supplies stored, Duncan put the triple-bagged rat in the break room trash can, then headed up front.

"Cyrus," I said to the air, as I washed my hands for the third time, "you can show up any time here. I really need your help."

No answer. We'd see if he would pop in later in the day. For now, it was time to get through the morning routine. First things first, though, I made myself a note to bring the rat home after we closed. The last thing I needed was a rat stinking up the store.

Uncle Cyrus or not, I realized I had resources to call on here in the shop itself. I left Duncan at the front counter and headed to the back corner toward the occult and paranormal section.

"Hey, Biff," I said, "are you around?"

The ghost of the former proprietor appeared as a hazy mist in front of me.

::*You rang?*:: he asked.

"Very funny, Lurch. What do you know about ghouls?"

"Ghouls?" A voice squeaked from above me. I looked up. It was Posey, one of our two resident gargoyles, perched on a tall bookcase. His friend Petal was on the bookcase opposite. "What do you want with ghouls?"

The larger question was, what did the ghouls want with me?

I updated both of the gargoyles and the ghost.

"So, I think we need to stake out the cemetery again. Last night was a bust."

The gargoyles both squeaked, "You can't do that!"

Biff looked horrified. ::*The revenants will eat you!*::

"I don't think these are those kinds of revenants," I said. "They seem pretty harmless."

::*Ghouls are never harmless,*:: Biff said. ::*If you want my help, you must promise to do no such thing.*::

Biff crossed his ghostly arms over his pot belly.

"Okay. I promise. At least for now."

I was kind of hoping he wouldn't notice that last part.

The ghost sniffed. ::*Forever.*::

"I can't promise that, but I can promise to be very careful. And to not stake out cemetery unless it feels absolutely necessary."

The ghost huffed.

::Fine. I'll help you. But you'd better make yourself a cup of tea and sit down. This is going to take a while.::

I made myself tea in record time, delivering a cup to Duncan while I was at it. I wished the teens were here to take notes and ask questions. In a short time, I'd come to rely on those two for research, and to pick up on angles I might otherwise miss.

But teenagers had to go to school, darn them.

Soon enough, I was ensconced in the comfy reading chair in what we called Biff's Corner. The two gargoyles were perched on the bookcases forming aisles up to the front of the shop, and Biff hovered nearby, clearly distressed.

::Ghouls are tricky,:: he began.

I breathed across the surface of my English Breakfast with oat milk and half a teaspoon of sugar. After this morning's events, I needed a bit of sweetness.

"Tricky how?" Petal asked from above my shoulder.

::Some of them seem nice at first, but the reality is, they all feast on dead things. They rob graves and terrify families.::

"Ghouls rob graves? That doesn't make sense to me," I said. "I mean, aren't they part of what we class as the undead?"

Biff shook his head vehemently and flapped his hands. He began to flicker in and out of presence, another sign he was upset.

::Ghouls are not zombies. Or vampires. Or any of the rest. Ghouls are made.::

I set my mug down on the top of the low bookcase to my right.

"What do you mean made? Vampires are made, aren't they?"

"Werewolves, too!" said Posey.

Biff frowned at me. ::*I thought your parents taught you better, Sarah. Magical beings of all sorts can be created by other magical beings, for good or ill.*::

Now it was my turn to frown.

"You mean like egregores?"

Biff's ghostly face lit up. Literally. He grew three shades brighter.

No pun intended.

::*Yes!*:: the ghost shouted in my head.

"What's an egregore? Sounds strange," asked Petal, her little stone face scrunched up in question.

I settled back in my chair, took a big gulp of milky tea, and tried to think of how to explain such things.

"Egregores are created by a person or group of people. Sometimes we do it consciously, and other times, unconsciously."

"I don't get it," said Posey.

"Let's say there are two gargoyles who are really good friends. Together, they create another energy being that is the relationship between the two of them. Groups do this, too. Every community has an energy body that attaches to the culture the community forms together. It can help things run smoothly, or it can also trip things up. Make it hard to change."

I looked up at the shelf tops to see if the stone creatures were following. They both looked confused, but Biff was nodding his head with excitement.

"And other times, a magician can create an egregore to do her bidding. For example, she can use an egregore to influence people's thoughts or actions. She can incite a crowd to become a mob. Or she can ensure that people entering her store have a pleasant experience."

::*Or....*:: Biff prompted.

"Or," I continued, realization truly dawning, "she can bind together grief, anger, love, and rage into an entity that haunts gravesides. And that being can feed off any life that wanders by in order to strengthen itself."

"Sounds scary," said Petal.

"It can be, though it doesn't have to be." I sat back in my chair again. "Unless the magician loses control of the egregore and it goes rogue."

And I was terrified that we were dealing with a rogue ghoul. But who had made it?

And how long ago?

8

The curtains covering the huge picture windows that were the selling point of Stefon's apartment were closed against the gloomy autumn evening outside. I sat on his comfy L-shaped sofa staring at the ultra-modern black-framed electric fire that levitated in the wall beneath his large screen television and gaming consoles.

My tall, beefy knight of a boyfriend was just in view behind the breakfast bar that separated the main living room from his kitchen. The kitchen was also top of the line, which was good, because Stefon loves to cook, and I love to eat his cooking.

He wore baggy jeans, his favorite *Sisko is My Captain* T-shirt, and a black hoodie with flaming twenty-sided dice on the back. He moved gracefully from sink, to counter, to stovetop, whipping up salmon and vegetables. I could smell the rice in its little cooker.

My stomach growled, but I contented myself with a

sip of hot mint tea from the mug cradled between both my hands. It was a Bookshop Witch mug, some more swag from the shop, brainstormed by my marketing mavens, Tracy and Tabitha.

I loved it more than I admitted.

"So, ghouls, huh?" Stefon said, turning the cooking vegetables in the pan before clicking off the gas. Stefon had what I lacked in the kitchen, which was timing.

I could make the heck out of soup, stews, or salads, but food that required different dishes cooking properly when they required different times? Not so much.

"Yes. Ghouls. And revenants. And egregores. And dead rats."

He shook his head, mouth turned down in a slight frown in the middle of the thicket of his soft, curly brown, almost black, beard. His hair and beard were two shades darker than his skin, framing his beautiful eyes and lips, and making me want to drag him onto the couch and kiss him all night.

After dinner, of course.

I'd much rather be kissing Stefon than discussing dead rats.

"Those rats worry me," he said. "Who is warning you, and why?"

"That's what we can't figure out. It seems like ghouls, but both rats were left during the daytime. Plus, Main Street seems a bit far from the cemetery for ghouls to travel."

Stefon began to plate the food. I moved to the kitchen to get out cutlery and two cloth napkins from his stash. That's another good thing about dating a man who plays at medieval reenactment: they always use cloth napkins. My ex, Cecilia, bless her, is a mechanic, and eating at her place always meant paper towels ripped from the roll. Now that she's partnered with a hob, her kitchenwares game has improved, at least.

Soon, we were seated at the breakfast bar on the big, high stools that fit my frame well, because they fit Stefon's much larger frame. It was nice dating someone bigger than me for once, just because the furniture was so dang comfortable.

I forked a piece of perfectly cooked salmon into my mouth and moaned. "Dill?" I asked when I could speak again.

"Dill and olive oil," he replied, then kissed the corner of my mouth. "Mmm. You're right. Delicious."

I swatted him with my napkin and a warm laugh rumbled from his luscious, round belly.

"You asked Liam or Tetris about it?"

I chewed some broccolini and leek—also delicious—and swallowed before answering.

"Haven't had time. I needed to get to the old graveyard before opening today. Serafina was the one who said it probably wasn't ghouls."

Stefon put his fork down and turned to look at me directly. "What exactly was a centaur doing in the cemetery? I thought you said their territory was just outside of town. In the woods."

He had a point. I'd been so caught up in my own rumination, I forgotten to follow up on how weird that was.

"I mean, centaurs do come into town sometimes. You've seen them."

"Doesn't it seem a bit convenient though? That she appeared right when you were at the old cemetery no one visits except a few Goth teens?"

Goth teens like Tabitha, who was at school during the time frame in question.

Now it was my turn to set down my fork, and I wasn't happy about it.

"You're supposed to be helping me answer my questions, not raise more red flags," I groused.

"Sorry, babe. I just call it like I see it."

"And I hate that you're right."

We picked up our forks and ate in silence for a few minutes.

"You know, in D&D, ghouls roam in packs, seeking out flesh to eat. They rip people apart, mindlessly. They don't drain rats and leave them as warnings on people's doorsteps."

"What are you saying?"

"I mean, I know it's just a game, but in D&D? Ghouls don't warn. They just kill."

"Ugh. Why are we having this conversation during dinner?"

"Babe. You know you can't take a night off until you get this figured out. So, I'm gonna ask you again: When you gonna talk with other folks in town? That tarot guy? Liam? Some of the others? You know everyone in town will help."

Except the ones leaving the warnings, maybe.

"You're the second person to tell me I need to check in at The Kelpie," I finally said. "But to talk to the ghosts, not Liam."

"It's a good idea, but I think you also need to talk to as many humans as you can."

"And why is that?"

"Because in my experience? Humans are the most dangerous creatures of all."

9

I t was a drippy October morning, and I was walking to the Blueberry Café for my muffin and tea fix when Tetris hailed me from across the street, waving his arms as if we were ships and he was semaphoring.

I glanced at my watch. I would have enough time to get tea and a muffin to go, but not enough time to sit and talk to Angie and talk to Tetris, too. One more look at his face made my decision for me. I waved a hand back to let him know I'd seen him.

He nodded and lowered his arms. I looked both ways and crossed the street. Luckily, I didn't have to wait for traffic, it being October. Crossing Main Street in high season was an excitement-filled, death-defying obstacle course. Autumn was a nice break from the traffic.

Further down the street, Roddy Devall was opening up his shop. Roddy was a skinny, flashy white guy who tried to dress like Uncle Cyrus and failed, unlike the distinguished looking man with the pale, silvery hair and fabulous long wool coat waited patiently. I looked more closely. It was the same man I'd seen in the Blueberry Cafe. I wondered if he was new in town. If so, it looked as if he was planning on buying or renting a place.

Or he was dating Roddy, a thought which made me shudder. Roddy was too odious for the likes of anyone, let alone someone like the man at his side.

In small towns, the LGBTQ community usually sticks together, but no one really liked Roddy. Case in point were my ex, Cecilia, and her boss, Raul. They hated it when Roddy needed his car looked at. He was always flirting with Raul, then dropping broad hints that the shop was "sitting on a piece of prime real estate. Shame to waste it on old cars, really."

So, yeah, Roddy Devall was not the most popular addition to our happy little Seashell Cove family. But something was bugging me about seeing them together. I wondered if Roddy and the strange man were up to something.

Probably just me seeing suspects behind every bush.

I walked toward Ancient Treasures.

"Tetris, what's up?"

The aging punk rocker looked disturbed. That was becoming a theme among pretty much everyone I encountered in Seashell Cove these days.

"I have something to show you," he said. "I'll be quick. I know you have to open shop, and I do, too. Come on through."

After locking the door behind us, he led me through the warren of display cases filled with fossils and bones, and shelves filled with dinosaur plushies, books, and everything that a dinosaur-loving adult or child would be inclined to buy. Which reminded me...

"I didn't hear the T-Rex roar when you opened the door this morning."

He shook his head sadly. "I'm too stressed out right now to deal with the noise."

Okay, this was the side of Tetris I hadn't seen before. Usually he was pretty chill, but his slim shoulders were hunched beneath an old concert hoodie from Ministry that he must've gotten in the nineties.

Tetris took good care of his clothing. I'll give him that.

I followed him through a second doorway, back to where his stockroom was. We passed a washroom and a tiny kitchen and kept going towards a back exit.

He pushed through a steel door and pointed.

"There," he said.

"Oh no," I replied, looking down at the oily tarmac and trying not to breathe too deeply because the alleyway was lined with big trash cans that clearly hadn't been picked up yet this week.

But stinky trash cans were the least of my worries, considering that yet another dead rat lay on a rotting banana peel.

"I heard about Angie," he said, "and thought you should see this."

"Were your windows, painted, too?"

He nodded. "Yeah, looked like blood."

A gleam caught my eye. Something was in the dead rat's mouth.

"Tetris. Do you see that?"

"See what? It's the rat."

"No. In its mouth."

He squatted down, hands on the knees of his faded, no-longer-black jeans and leaned over the rat. I stood well back, not caring to get too close if I didn't have to. I'd had quite enough of the other rats, thank you.

"Dang. You're right. Got a pencil? Pen?"

"No."

He patted his pockets and dug out a set of keys with a small multitool on the ring.

"Tweezers!" he crowed, as if he'd just found a rare fossil among the garbage.

I watched as he oh-so-carefully dipped the tweezers into the rat's mouth and drew out a small key. And not just any old key. It looked antique, all tarnished silver curlicues with a heavy, three-pronged end that slotted into an old-fashioned keyhole. It looked like something one of the antique shops that dotted the coast would have in a basket near the register. An impulse buy for folks who liked old stuff.

Or the kind of thing one of Stefon's D&D quest followers would use to open a treasure box found in the dungeon of some ancient keep.

Or—I shivered inside my Widening Gyre hoodie— the sort of key that would open a magical grimoire that should remain closed.

"Maybe that's why someone keeps painting 'Beware' all over."

"Huh?" Tetris stood, still staring down at the key, almost as if hypnotized.

I hadn't realized I'd spoken aloud, and wasn't really ready to share any theories with Tetris yet. I had to consult with Carol and Delta first, and maybe Jerry Hamamoto.

And I really need to talk with Cyrus.

Where had he gotten to? He was always leaving in the middle of things!

"Nothing," I replied. "Just thinking out loud. "Do you have a baggie to put that in?"

Tetris gave me a look that telegraphed exactly what he thought of my little fib, though he didn't comment, just nodded and opened the door again.

I was soon sorted with the key in a small plastic bag with a sealed top and was headed to Angie's to pick up a muffin. By now I really was late. I could make tea at the bookshop, thank all the Gods and Goddesses.

A plan formed in my head as I said my goodbyes and headed back across Main.

This needed all hands on deck, because a dead rat was bad enough, but a rat with a silver key in its mouth? That spelled out magic, loud and clear.

And strange magic and warnings this close to Halloween?

Made my blood run cold.

10

Before the meeting started at The Historic Kelpie, there was something I needed to do. I stood in the little bar area sandwiched between the lobby and the dining room. Like the rest of The Kelpie, the bar was floor to ceiling with weird art and decorations, and bright bottles lined the back of the bar itself.

"Bunny?" I called. "You around?"

The flapper popped into view right next to me, a sparkle in her eye that matched the rhinestone fascinator in her bobbed hair. She wore a fringed dress and T-strap shoes, as always. Bunny was a lot more solid looking than when we'd first met. I guess having living humans see you made you want to show up more. Made sense to me.

::Hi Sarah! What do you need? Did the meeting start already?::

"Not yet. But I needed to ask if you or any of the other ghosts have heard grumblings about things going wrong in the graveyard. Or know anything about dead rats."

I crossed my fingers that she wouldn't be insulted, but she just seemed confused, wrinkling her ghostly brow.

::Dead rats? How disgusting! And we Kelpie ghosts don't have much to do with the graveyard ghosts. The ones that are awake are kind of old fuddy duddies. They don't like to have a good time, you know?::

I nodded, as if I understood completely. I was a little disappointed. I thought for sure the Kelpie ghosts would know something about what was going on.

"Well, if you hear anything, you let me know. I guess we should head into the dining room." I could hear noises coming from the room next door, which told me everyone had arrived, and so should I.

Bunny glided behind me into the big dining room, and sure enough, our friends were gathering around the large communal table in the center of the room, with a few spilling out into the booths along the walls and windows.

A soft rain pattered outside, and Sophie—her fading blond hair tied back in a ponytail—bustled about, helping Liam serve tea or soda water. Tabitha and Tracy pitched in, too. The rest of us sat around the long communal table with its mismatched fancy chairs, including Carol, Uncle Cyrus, and Ah Lam Wu.

Jerry and Ash Hamamoto sat across from me, next to the two warlocks, while Carol took one end chair. Delta and Preston were at the opposite end.

Stefon, of course, was at my side, his muscular thigh pressing against mine.

::You must have a Halloween party here,:: Bunny said, practically dancing next to Delta's chair. The ghostly flapper bounced in her T-strap shoes with glee, the

fringes and beads on her party gown shimmering and swinging.

"It's not a party," Delta grumbled. "Or its not meant to be. It's a Samhain observance. A time to commune with the dead. That's a serious undertaking."

Bunny wrinkled her button nose in confusion. ::*Crikey! Why so glum? What do the dead like more than a party?*::

I burst out laughing, and Stefon elbowed me in the side.

"What's happening?"

"You remember Bunny, the flapper?"

He nodded.

"She wants a party for Samhain. Says that's exactly what the dead want. And Delta?"

Delta just shook her head in disgust.

"I guess Delta doesn't think that's a very good idea," I finished.

"Hmm. I'm with Bunny," Stefon said. "I love a good party."

"Yes, you do, my nerdy, extroverted friend."

I gave him a quick kiss, and he gave me a squeeze back.

Finally, everyone had the beverage of their choice, but the teens were still bustling with snacks.

Liam sat and looked around expectantly. The Irish American innkeeper with his blue eyes and pale skin and hair was one of those aging handsome types. I bet he looked like a movie star when he was in his twenties.

"What's this about a party?" he said. "If there's a party to be had, we should definitely have it here. How many people are we talking?"

"It's not a party," Delta grumped again.

"Delta," Carol said, "you might have to give that over. If we're gathering to honor the dead, and the dead of Seashell Cove want to party? I think the party we shall have."

"Oh, wicked," Tabitha said. "That's perfect! A Samhain party!"

I cleared my throat and waited until everyone looked my way. "Can we save the party planning for later? We have other business to attend to this evening."

"Oh, right!" Tracy said. The teens flung their snacks onto the table, then scurried and scooted out chairs and plopped their skinny butts down.

Okay. Everyone was accounted for now.

Except there was a thumping at the door leading into the small courtyard off the dining room. Liam leaped up to open it. It was Serafina and Máni.

The two centaurs couldn't have been less alike. One had a coal black coat and the other was as pale as the moon he was named for.

"We heard there was a meeting," Serafina said, "and wondered why we were not invited."

"It, it..." I stammered. "It was ad hoc! Planned at the last minute. We were going to tell you once we had figured some more things out."

"You can tell us now," Serafina said, trotting around to an open spot at the table. Máni clopped behind her. They were both amazingly beautiful and still startling to me, almost taking my breath away.

When Serafina wasn't scaring the snot out of me.

At any rate, I hoped I never became so used to the

beauty of magic that I forgot to register how special it was.

"So, you all know about the drained rats and the threatening messages. But the thing you don't know..." I unwrapped the ornate key from a scrap of silk. "Is that we found this in the rat behind Tetris's shop."

Ah Lam Wu leaned forward, her tiny nose sniffing the air. I could see her fingers twitching as if they wanted to grasp the thing.

I shoved it across the table towards her and Uncle Cyrus.

"I was hoping the two of you had some idea what this was. And why it would be found in a drained rat's mouth."

"A key?" Angie said. "Why would someone stuff a key inside a rat?"

"And then kill the rat?" Tetris finished. "Or vice versa?"

"Those are very good questions," said Angelica, stroking the air above the key, her perfectly manicured purple nails flashing in the overhead lights.

"I've heard of such artifacts," said Jerry Hamamoto.

"You have, Dad?" Ash took out a notebook, ready to write down everything. The boy was taking a leaf out of Tracy and Tabitha's book, and that was a good thing.

"Well, psychopomps hold the keys to the afterlife, so it makes sense to me that a key would be found inside a dead thing," Cyrus said.

"You mean it's a message?" Tracy asked.

He nodded. "It looks that way to me, although I defer to the warlocks of the council here."

Uncle Cyrus shook his head. "We warlocks of the

council welcome input from others who have studied the magical arts. And you may be right, this may very well be the work of a psychopomp. But we still do not know why."

He turned to his colleague and maybe girlfriend, who turned the key over in her hands.

"Are you getting anything?" he asked.

Ah Lam shook her head, dark hair swishing around her delicate face.

"I am but I can't *quite* read it. Not yet. It might be that there are too many magical beings around for me to get a clear signal."

"We thought it was ghouls at first," Delta said, "except the rats were all left during the daytime and it has also been pointed out that ghouls travel in packs."

Which would make them a bit hard to miss, wandering down Main Street.

Ah Lam nodded. "Yes, I can see why you thought it was a ghoul."

"From your description of the drained animals, it could be that someone is using the ghouls, taking their leavings as it were," Uncle Cyrus said, "and using them to warn you and throw you off the scent."

"But why?" Tabitha asked. We all looked at her.

"That's the question of the hour," I said. "I wish I knew."

"And warn us about what?" Tracy chimed in.

"We have noticed strange goings-on at the cemetery and have been trying to ascertain what the trouble is," Serafina remarked.

I felt the flush of anger rise in me. "And why didn't you tell us that before? The day I met you there?"

Máni held up placating hands. "We were not yet certain and did not wish to cause undue alarm or speculation."

I crossed my arms over my chest and bit my tongue. What the pale centaur said made a certain amount of sense, but that didn't mean I wasn't miffed.

Stefon patted my knee in understanding. It was a sympathetic gesture, but also one that told me to keep my cool.

"What sort of goings-on?" Tabitha asked.

"Gatherings at night," Máni said.

"Flickering candles. Incantations," Serafina continued. "Strange chanting."

"And giggling. Don't forget the giggling," Máni interjected.

"Sounds like a coven," Tabitha remarked. "Actually, sounds a lot like some of the wannabe Wiccans at school."

"Come on, Tabitha," her friend said, "you really think those kids would be leaving drained rats on people's doorsteps?"

Tabitha shrugged. "Probably not. But the two things don't have to be connected, the rats and the ghouls and the strange sights and sounds in the cemetery. Do they?"

I groaned. Great. Just what we needed: two mysteries to solve.

"Were you able to get close enough to see these people?" Tetris asked. "Do we need to do a stakeout?"

Serafina shook her head. "We did not want to approach too closely in case they were ordinary humans."

Well, that made sense. Even though Seashell Cove

was known to be a bit uncanny by now, and The Kelpie Inn—and more recently, my bookshop—cashed in on the whole haunted aspect, people were still blissfully unaware that things like centaurs and gnomes and dryads and the like actually existed, let alone witches and warlocks that had nothing to do with contemporary pagan practices.

"Back to the rats," I said.

"Back to the party," Delta said in the same breath.

"Delta!" I snapped, irritated at the older witch. "I know you think the Samhain gathering is important. But don't you think we ought to solve the case of the drained rats first?"

She shook her head, tousled gray hair becoming spinier by the moment. She looked like a deranged hedgehog.

"We have to act as if all of these things are connected. Until we can prove they aren't."

I looked at Cyrus and Ah Lam Wu in exasperation. Cyrus stroked his chin and Ah Lam Wu tapped purple-painted fingernails on the table.

"I think Delta is right," Ah Lam finally said. "In our training, we have to act as if there are no coincidences, yet keep an open mind that things might not be connected at all."

That is so not my specialty. I either want to know what the connections are, or I want to deal with things one at a time. But they were right, so I shut my trap.

"So, what do we do next?" Stefon asked.

::Why don't you leave the party planning to me?:: Bunny said. *::I can get all the ghosts here on board. All you all have to do is work on invitations.::*

"How are you going to prepare food?" Sophie asked, hands on her hips. Bunny looked crestfallen. Sophie was the cleaner for The Inn, and had helped us on cases in the past.

::Oh, that. Could you and Liam help?::

Sophie looked at Liam, who raised an eyebrow.

"Here's what I think," Sophie said. "Delta, if you're willing to work with me on this, you, Bunny, and the ghosts and I can plan this thing, right? And Liam can help us with the food and drinks."

Delta made a grumbling noise in her throat, clearly feeling railroaded, but nodded in agreement. That was a relief. I did not have time to deal with all of this and plan the first ever Seashell Cove Samhain event.

"All right," I said. "Why don't we break into small groups? Party planners can meet in the bar, and the rest of us can continue strategizing here."

Delta threw me a resentful glance.

"Delta, if you want to be part of this strategy meeting, I bet Sophie and Bunny can catch you up later."

The older witch looked mollified at that. The last thing I wanted was for Delta Crabbit to feel as if I was leaving her out of this investigation.

I had learned that being Justice takes a village, and I would hate to alienate one of my key supporters and assets.

"Sure, we can do that," Sophie said, patting Delta on the shoulder. "No problem."

That was a relief. "All right. Let's take a short break and then get back to work."

11

We had met for another hour at The Kelpie and gotten a start on the party planning. Dealing with the rats and all? Not so much. I'd had a restless night's sleep, dreaming of my mother, holding out a large, magical book and a silver key. She was pointing to the book, entreating me with big eyes to please understand.

Except I didn't understand. I just woke up with a headache that took two aspirin, the pounding hot water of a shower on the back of my neck, and a cup of tea to dissipate.

So here I was, back at The Widening Gyre, large second mug of tea close to hand, trying to unravel what my message my mother was trying to give me.

It was a Saturday, and I really needed to focus on the shop. Even though it was October, things would be busier than during the week. Besides which, I had a business to run, accounts to keep, stock to check in, used books to go through, and space to make on the shelves for new arrivals. So, here I was behind the front desk, Stevie Nicks queued up on the sound system.

What can I say? When your parents name you after a Stevie Nicks song, and your cat is named Rhiannon, Stevie Nicks was what you get five times out of ten.

Rhiannon was napping in the window, the Petal and Posey were gargoyle-ing, perched on top of the tall bookcases that ran along the center aisle and side walls of the shop, and Biff was doing whatever ghosts do on their off time.

And me? I was happily humming along to Stevie's warble, getting a crack at the box of used books Duncan had bought the day before.

There were some good ones. Old fantasy books, science fiction, historical romance. A few biographies, some poetry, and books on political theory. The combination made me want to meet whomever the books had come from. They were clearly a person with a wide variety of interests.

I was reaching in for another book when the shop door jangled, and in walked Ash and Jerry Hamamoto. Ash rushed up to the counter, dark eyes alight in his slightly elfin face, the one tell that when the boy had been born, everyone in the hospital thought he was a girl. Luckily, he had a dad who understood Ash's real nature.

"Hi Sarah!" Ash said. "I brought the reviews."

He slapped four slips of paper on the countertop.

"Thanks, Ash. Let's see what you got here."

I leafed through them, looking at the reviews the boy had written out neatly, on index cards cut in half, designed to fit on the edges of a bookcase. When Ash and his dad first moved to town, I could tell they were a bit short on cash, offered to give Ash any of the used children's books he wanted in exchange for these neatly printed shelf talkers. The boy happily complied.

The arrangement warmed my heart and gave Ash all the reading material he wanted with a larger selection than our small-town library had, and customers appreciated the reviews.

I flipped through the cards and smiled.

"These look great. Thanks."

"Whatcha doing?" Ash asked.

His father smiled. "I'll leave you two to it. I want to browse a bit."

He sauntered down the aisle, his sneakers squeaking slightly on the old wood floors, likely heading toward one of four sections: psychology, occult and paranormal, religion, or thrillers.

"I'm unpacking books and stacking them into categories so we can price and shelve them."

"Can I help?"

"Sure, pull up a stool."

I waved him around the counter and got him settled. We worked together happily for a few minutes, me unboxing and him stacking. I reached in for a book at the very bottom of the box and felt a sharp prick.

"Ouch!" I stuck my finger in my mouth.

"What happened?"

"I'm not sure." I peered into the box and there was a leather tome that looked like it was covered in some sort of reptile skin. It was huge. Like complete-works-of-Shakespeare huge.

And it sported an oily-looking, encrusted lock. I swear the thing glowered at me.

Was this the book my mother had been showing me in my dream? Yuck!

Ash peered into the box, too, his small head next to mine.

"Whoa," he whispered. "What is that thing?"

"Ash? Would you go get your father, please?"

And Cyrus, I thought, *I could really use your help. Again.*

I sure as heck didn't want to take the thing out of the box without backup.

Mom, if you have any information on this thing, now's the time to tell me.

No voice. No vision. No nothing. Great. Sometimes being a witch means you have to do things yourself, doesn't it? But I really wished all I had to do was wave a wand.

As Ash scampered down the aisles, looking for his dad, I did a quick assessment. Who knows what nasties the book contained, and how that might affect me? My breathing was okay. Heart rate seemed fine. No tingling in my limbs.

Hopefully I hadn't been poisoned or magicked or whatever else happens when an ancient tome of unknown provenance bites your finger and you foolishly put it in your mouth.

Two sets of sneakers smacked their way back to the front, followed by the sound of creaking stone wings.

Ash and Jerry appeared from the center aisle, followed by the two gargoyles, who alighted atop the bookcase closest to the front desk.

"What's happening?" Jerry said, eyes concerned

beneath his wire-rimmed glasses. "Ash said something about a weird book?"

"Oh, it's weird all right. Take a look. But I wouldn't touch it if I were you."

Jerry's golden-hued skin turned pale. "That doesn't look like a friendly object."

"No kidding," I replied.

"What are we gonna do, Dad?"

"Got your uncle on speed dial?" Jerry asked me.

I shook my head. "You know him well enough by now. There's no telling where he is or when he'll show up."

He was probably canoodling with Ah Lam Wu. Not that I blamed him. She was smoking hot, and just his type.

"What are we gonna do?" Ash repeated.

Jerry and I both looked at the boy, then a creaking voice spoke from behind me.

"You need to call the ghouls," the Posey said.

"Call the ghouls?" I yelped. "How in the heck am I supposed to do that?"

The bells on the front door announced the arrival of Tracy and Tabitha.

As soon as I saw them, I knew what needed to happen next, but before I could get a word out, they burst into their usual enthusiastic chatter.

"We came to show you the new T-shirt designs we're cooking up," said Tabitha. The Asian teen was dressed in her usual Goth casual of black jeans, a black T-shirt with *Bad Witch* spelled out in a blue cursive font, a black anorak, and blue boots that matched the writing on the tee.

"I also designed a flier for the Samhain celebration!"

said Tracy, whose blond hair spilled over her burgundy winter jacket over dark blue jeans and black boots. Her T-shirt was one of her own designs, showing a ghost—Biff, if he looked like a puffy white cartoon—carrying a stack of books.

"That's great," I replied. "But we have something more urgent to discuss."

The teens stopped mid-stride and stared from me to Ash and Jerry, to Rhiannon on the counter and the gargoyles perched on the bookshelf.

No one said anything.

I gulped down some tea and trained my eyes on our resident Goth Wiccan.

"Tabitha, I hate to ask this of you, but Petal the gargoyle here says we need to call the ghouls."

She wrinkled her nose in confusion.

"Call the ghouls? Why do you think I know how to do that?"

Understanding dawned on her best friend's face. Tracy put a hand on Tabitha's arm and spoke gently.

"Tabitha, I think Sarah is asking if your parents would get involved."

Tabitha's normally pale gold skin lightened in fear and confusion.

"No. N-no." She flapped her hands in the air. "You can't ask me to. No."

Then she turned on her bootheel and ran out the door, bells clattering in her wake.

"That went well," Ash said.

I had no words in reply.

I looked down at the book on the counter. But at least

now I knew what my mother had been warning me about in the dream. There was something important about this book.

Now we just had to figure out what that was.

12

I was back at the cemetery.

It was nighttime and it was really the last place I wanted to be. But if Tabitha wouldn't ask her parents to intercede on my behalf, I decided I had to just pull up my big-girl panties and contact the ghouls myself.

At least that was the plan.

Stefon's reassuring bulk was beside me and Delta and Preston were having a quiet argument a few paces away.

"Stop crushing the herbs and salt!" Delta hissed in a whisper.

"What's it matter? They're already crushed!" Preston hissed back.

I rolled my eyes.

Stefon had insisted we needed to stick together, and he was right.

I wished we had more backup but also didn't feel right putting anyone else in possible danger. I didn't know ghouls and ghouls didn't know me. Tracy had wanted to come along, but I decided it was best if she and Carol tracked down Tabitha to make sure she was okay.

I hated upsetting the teen and had no idea that just the thought of me finally meeting her parents would cause that reaction. It had to be hard being a human teenager with parents who were vampires, especially in a small town like Seashell Cove.

I mean, did vampires even attend parent–teacher conferences? I couldn't imagine it.

"What's the next move, babe?" Stefon asked.

"Frankly, I don't know. We wander around. Or we pick a spot and wait. Do you have a preference?"

"I'd rather wander," he said.

I agreed. Movement always made me feel better, and I'd rather be a moving target than a sitting duck.

We threaded our way through the old headstones, some leaning to the side, others still standing straight and tall as the day they were placed.

Delta paced beside me, Preston bouncing along in her bag. His little head and purple hat kept sticking up out of the top of the bag, eyes with amazement or fear, I couldn't tell which.

We circled around towards the edges, away from the large spruce at the center of the cemetery. At least my eyes had adjusted to the dim light, so I wasn't going to crack my knee on a headstone. I hoped.

The cemetery was lit only by a streetlamp at the opposite corner of the park. That was one reason I was sticking to the edges. The center by the spruce was dark, and gloomy as anything. Who knew what lurked there?

I really didn't feel like risking it. Not yet. I had the

book safely zipped up in a backpack, and the key in my pocket, just in case. I hoped I wouldn't have to use either.

"Oh no," Preston said, his voice quavering.

"What's the matter Preston?" Delta groused. "Have to pee?"

"No." The gnome sounded very offended. "I do not have to *pee*. I am not a child."

"Then what?"

I swear, those two were like the proverbial old married couple. Always sniping.

"I think I see something right there." The gnome pointed. "Over by that headstone."

"Which headstone?" Stefon asked, his head swiveling.

And then I saw it. At the base of an obelisk.

A dead rat. Great.

"Preston's right. There's a drained rat just ahead." I walked swiftly towards it, not watching my step, and cracked my shin on a tumbled-down gravestone.

"Ouch! Dang it," I said, hopping on one foot, sucking in air, hissing in pain.

"Babe," Stefon said, putting an arm around me. "Chill out."

"You crack your shin bone on a headstone and see how you like it!" I said.

He patted my back. "Sorry. I think we're all a little on edge."

I gingerly placed my foot back on the ground.

"You okay to walk?" he asked.

"Yes," I said, shoving away from him.

Petty, I know. But he was right. This place was seriously giving me the creeps.

The Goth teenager I used to be would have been

horrified that I was creeped out wandering the grave site in the dark, but sheesh! I mean, we did use to picnic here, but that was on sunny afternoons, not ten o'clock on an October night.

I bent down to examine the rat. It looked deflated, as if disappointed that its life had led it here.

"It looks the same as the others," I said, "drained of blood and life force."

"What are you doing heeeere?" a strange voice said.

And by strange, I mean unearthly, otherworldly, spectral. You know, all those adjectives one uses when talking about the undead.

"Who's there?" Delta asked.

I heard the ring of steel being drawn.

"Stefon? You brought a knife?" I whispered.

"Babe. You think I was coming to a graveyard at night with no weapons? What am I, nuts?"

"Well, you have a point there."

He held out the knife towards the wavering figure behind the headstone. It was ugly. Like terrifyingly ugly.

The ghoul—because there was nothing else it could be—looked like a strange cross between a decaying body, a demon, and a ghost. It wasn't classic zombie, despite the decay. It had glowing red eyes, the way I imagined a demon would, though I pray to Hecate Goddess of Witches that I never meet one. But there was also a spectral aura around its body, the way all ghosts I've ever met have. That misty, greenish glow that old-school spiritualists used to call ectoplasm.

It moved more quickly than a classic zombie, too, which was not to our advantage.

"I repeat," it hissed, "what are you doing heeeere? You

do not belong in sssuch a place. You have not been invited to our home."

"Your home?" I asked. "I thought this was the home for the dead. You don't look dead to me."

"Sarah," Delta hissed, poking me in the ribs to shut me up. Yeah, sometimes my mouth gets away from me. But what can I say?

The thing laughed. At least, I think it was a laugh. You ever heard someone from the water department drag a cover off a storm drain? The way it grates across the concrete?

Yeah, the ghoul's laugh was a little like that.

"Sarah," Stefon's voice was urgent. "We've got company."

Preston the gnome squeaked and dove back into his tote bag. Delta's head whipped around to look at the cemetery. I turned more slowly, taking it all in, suddenly grateful for Stefon's knife and for whatever herbs and salt Delta was rummaging for in the tote. At least, I hoped that's what she was doing.

Though whether herbs and salt worked to ward off ghouls, I didn't know.

"Delta?" I asked.

"Ready," she replied.

That was good, because we were surrounded. Ghouls emerged from behind headstones all around us, and every last one was headed our way.

"This is so not good," I mumbled.

"You think?" Stefon replied. "I hope you have a plan."

He knew I didn't. I knew I didn't.

I just hoped my witch's intuition did.

The ghouls moved toward us, some shambling

calmly, others, darting from grave to grave. There were tall ghouls, and short ghouls, wide ghouls, and slender ghouls.

"And even kind and tender ghouls," I sang softly into the night.

"Sarah! Have you taken leave of your senses?" Delta snapped.

Uh. Maybe.

"Sorry," I replied, bracing my sturdy black hiking boots against the grass. "Just nervous."

I slowed my breathing down, trying to calm the butterflies flinging themselves against each other inside my belly.

"You got this, babe," Stefon murmured, brushing the back of my hand with his. But I noticed he moved carefully, in a martial arts stance, center low, head on swivel.

The ghouls stepped closer and closer, until I could smell them, and let me tell you, ghouls smell disgusting. Like summer roadkill, grave dirt, and microwaved fish disgusting.

I coughed, and retched, then took in a heaving breath through my mouth. I could hear Preston and Delta coughing, too. Stefon seemed impervious, dang him.

Eyes watering, I straightened my spine, and calling on all my authority as Justice, I raised my voice.

"Halt! Stop! Come no further!" I held my right hand, palm out, toward the first ghoul.

"Or what?" The ghoul laughed that awful laugh again, the sound clawing at my backbone.

"Or I will destroy the book!"

I had no idea what prompted me to say that, but it served to confuse the ghouls enough that they actually paused, giving us a sliver of much-needed breathing room.

"Sarah," Stefon leaned toward me, keeping his voice low, "incoming."

He jerked his head toward the outer edge of the cemetery, the portion closest to the cliffs, with their sheer drop to the ocean.

The air currents shifted, and where all I could smell before was ghoul, I caught a hint of ocean, grass, and something that smelled very familiar.

The scent that caught me was that of old paper, just beginning to decay. It reminded me of the antiquarian bookshops my dad sometimes took me to as a child. Those places were wonderlands filled mostly with things I was not allowed to touch. We would spend an hour there and leave with the scent clinging to our clothing.

Underneath the papery smell was the tang of old blood.

I froze. Could these be our rat-dropping blood-writing culprits?

The ghouls hissed and growled, clattering their teeth and moving their limbs in a creepy, disjointed way. And they all turned toward the cliffs, where two figures slowly rose into the air.

And by "rose into the air," I mean literally. They weren't flying, exactly, or floating. No. It was more like levitation.

"How the Hades are they doing that?" Stefon whispered.

Wouldn't we all like to know?

Meanwhile, the two figures moved steadily toward us. The closer they got, the more I could see they looked like two ordinary, middle-aged people, dressed in the standard Pacific Northwest uniform of heavy rain jackets, hoods resting on their back, jeans, and boots. They looked Asian American to me. The woman had long, stick-straight black hair, a small nose, and slightly tilted eyes. The man's hair was dark, but shot with silver that caught the streetlamp. He smiled, but it didn't look very friendly.

I just hoped whatever that emotion was, he was feeling it for the ghouls, and not for our little band.

They also glowed bluishwhite, just a little bit around the edges.

"What are they? Delta?"

She barked out a soft laugh.

"You know how you've been wanting to meet Tabitha's parents?"

I turned to the shorter witch in confusion. "Yeah? So?"

"Come on, Sarah!" she replied. "What do you think vampires look like?"

13

"Oh, my Gods and Goddesses!" I yelped.

A bit too loudly, I guess, because every head in the cemetery turned to look at me. Some heads turned a full three-sixty and back again—Linda Blair style—which let me tell you is creepy as anything, and something I hope to never witness again.

The hovering woman laughed this time, and it sounded like a real, human laugh.

"You must be Sarah Braxton," she said. "We've heard so much about you."

The two vampires levitated just behind the first ghoul, who did not look pleased. I made a note to ask about vampire-ghoul relations at some point in the future.

"Have you come to help?" Preston asked, his little face peeking just above the top of the tote bag.

The male vampire spoke this time. "We heard you might be here tonight, and figured we'd offer assistance as a go-between, if necessary."

"Or physical backup," Tabitha's mother interjected, spearing the lead ghoul with a look that, if it couldn't kill, could at least maim. Then she smiled sweetly. "If necessary."

Wow. Okay. Tabitha's 'rents looked like ordinary middle-aged people but were actually kind of badass. I just hoped they could do what they said.

I cleared my throat.

"We came here to ask if anyone knows about threats being lobbied at various people around Seashell Cove. We don't appreciate messages being painted in blood on our shop windows, possibly scaring off tourists."

The lead ghoul raised its hands and shrugged. "Thessse were left in daylight hoursss, were they not?"

"Yes," I replied.

"Ghoulsss cannot walk while the sun is in the skyyy," it said simply.

"But the drained rats..." Delta said.

"A ghoul must take in sssustenance. Is it our fault that someone stole our leavingsss from this place?"

The ghoul's words were very reasonable but left a bad taste in my mouth that had nothing to do with the smell.

Well, almost nothing.

Something felt off about this whole situation.

A second ghoul looked at me from the corner of its eyes, a sly grin on its decaying face.

"We did hear you found an intriguing book today. But why would you wisssh to dessstroy it? Hmmm? And why do you think weee would care?"

"Where are you getting your information?" Stefon asked, drawing himself up to his full height and girth. I couldn't see it, but I swear it sounded like he flexed his muscles.

"Good question," I said, realizing what had felt off earlier. How did the ghouls know the vandals had struck during daylight hours? We had not told them. Someone was feeding them information.

My backpack felt suddenly heavy, and the book, not so well hidden anymore. The key in my front pocket felt conspicuous, too, as if anyone could see its outline through the dark denim.

That's just your paranoia talking, Sarah. I willed myself to not adjust my backpack, and not pat my pockets.

But despite my reassurances to myself, I couldn't help but feel that the ghouls knew exactly what I carried into the cemetery, and why.

I only wished I knew why myself.

And I was really starting to wish that I'd come into the cemetery with a plan.

Half of the ghouls approached the hovering vampires, but the other half? They were moving towards us, which meant a greater threat, plus, wow, an increased stench that all the ocean breezes in the world could not waft away.

"What do we do?" I muttered to Stefon.

"Stay put," he said, "I got your back."

I guess he meant that literally, because he swung around behind me as Delta and Preston swung to my other side. We formed a little triangle, shoulder to shoulder, back to back. Able to see in all directions.

I still didn't feel good about it, but it was better than nothing. Like I said, no plan.

"What do you have in your backpack, witch? Isss it

the booook?" said ghoul number one. It was too close, and the rotting, microwaved-fish smell was almost overpowering.

Note to self: next time, spread some menthol chest rub under my nose before heading into the cemetery at night.

"Ever thought of using mouthwash?" I replied.

It hissed at me and lunged. I jerked back, bumping into Stefon and Delta.

"Show usss show usss what's in the backpack, Ssssaaarah?"

I hated that it knew my name. Ghouls are not the kind of people I want to be known by. I pushed off from Stefon's comforting bulk and forced myself to stand tall on my own two feet again.

"What makes you think I have anything in my backpack?"

"You said there was a book. And I am not a foooool," the ghoul hissed.

I fought down a gag at the stench.

"No. But you are a stinky ghoul," Stefon said.

I laughed, which meant I inhaled a huge whiff of ghoul, then coughed and gagged again.

The ghoul's face contorted into a rictus of anger and disgust. "You find the situation amusing?"

"Not particularly," I replied. "But it is kind of ridiculous."

Now I was just stalling for time. Over the first ghoul's shoulder, I could see the vampires fighting off the other creatures of the night. They were cutting quite a swath through them. If these two were really Tabitha's parents, they had quite the fighting chops. Like literally. They chopped through ghouls as if they carried swords, but they only used the sharp blades of their hands.

"Can you do that?" I turned my head to ask Stefon.

"Do what?"

"Chop up ghouls with just the sides of your hands?"

"Babe," he said.

Okay. Don't answer then.

"What's happening back there?" I asked over my shoulder.

"Not much," Delta replied. "Ghoul standoff at twenty paces."

Well, that was good. At least they weren't encroaching. But we couldn't stand here all night. My witch's intuition—or my general foolishness—decided it was time to take a risk.

"If I show you what's in my backpack, will you leave us alone?"

"Perhaps," said the ghoul.

"Not good enough," I replied.

The ghoul lunged again. I yelped, and Stefon whirled, jabbing at the ghoul with his long, gleaming knife.

My boyfriend is so badass.

He danced around the ghoul like the warrior that he is. By which I mean he sliced at the ghoul with one hand, dodged its decaying arms, and grabbed the thing's body with his other hand.

The ghoul didn't stand a chance and knew it. I could see it in his creepy eyes.

"Run!" he bellowed from his decaying throat.

The frenzy outside our tiny circle increased as the vampires fought their way through to us.

By the time they got there, the ghoul in Stefon's hands was dead.

I mean, I guess it was dead already, but you know, more dead.

Delta and I both looked at it, dangling from Stefon's big hand. He looked horrified, and as if he could not let the thing go.

"Stefon…" I started, and then watched the ghoul crumble into dust, leaving a pile of fresh soil at our feet. I took a sniff. Sure enough, the pile of dirt smelled like compost that had been cooking for a couple years, ready to spread around a vegetable garden. Oh, there was still a whiff of rotted fish, but mostly? The dead ghoul smelled okay. Like spring planting.

No wonder the cemetery was so green and beautiful. It wasn't just the city caretaker, it was dead bodies and ghouls.

The vampires touched down between two grave-stones. They didn't even look winded. Maybe if you didn't have a beating heart, your lungs work differently, too. Though they had to have lungs because they could speak, right?

"Sarah!" Delta elbowed me in the ribs.

"What?"

"Pay attention!"

"Oh, sorry. What did I miss?'

"Why did you come here?" said the male vampire.

"Reconnaissance?" That was definitely a question mark at the end of that word.

"Foolish witch," said the woman.

"I'm sorry," Stefon said, "I don't believe we've been introduced."

I could feel him drawing himself up to his full height and impressive breadth.

Finally, the vampires snapped out of it and stopped scowling.

"Our apologies," said the man, "we are, as you likely suspected, Tabitha's parents. My name is Andrew Huang, and this is my life partner, Lisa Zheng."

So. The undead can have life partners. Noted.

"I would say it's a pleasure to meet you, but given the circumstances? Not really." I shrugged. "Would you care to come back to my place for a cup of tea?"

Tabitha's mother, Lisa, gave a me genuine smile.

"That would be delightful," she said. "Lead on."

14

My living room was stuffed to the gills because we decided to get as many people at this meeting as possible.

So, Carol showed up with Tabitha and Tracy, and Liam came to represent The Kelpie. Tetris was there, too. Angie couldn't make it, which was unfortunate. But frankly, I had a feeling she was a bit traumatized by the whole situation and wanted to avoid it as much as possible.

I didn't blame her. I'd much rather be on a date with Stefon than in a meeting about dead rats. But a witch can't always choose, can she?

Tabitha threw glances at her parents, and looked pretty uncomfortable with the situation, but I was glad to have finally met them. They turned out to be really nice people. Even if they were vampires.

Looked like I was going to have to educate myself on what real vampires were like, instead of relying on steamy paranormal fantasy books and movies. After all, if everyone thought witches were the way the media portrayed us, my life would look a little different, wouldn't it?

En route home, I'd put out a psychic call to Uncle Cyrus, who had appeared post haste, for which I was grateful.

We were smushed on the sofa and chairs around the coffee table, with Tracy and Tabitha sitting on cushions on the floor. Preston and Rhiannon looked companionable on their shared cushion. Those two might have started off as rivals, but were forging an odd friendship.

I poured the promised tea into mismatched mugs. It was some soothing mint-with-a-dash-of-ginger blend in honor of the cool evening.

A fire snapped and crackled, fragrant with the scent of burning birch logs, making the room pleasantly warm, despite the chill that rose up my back every time I thought of my encounter with the ghouls.

From an armchair across the coffee table, Cyrus crossed his legs and steepled his fingers.

"You said you found this book in a box of donations?"

"Not donations," I said, handing mugs of tea to Tabitha's parents, who nodded their thanks. I'd see whether the vampires drank it or not, but they both seemed glad to cradle the warm mugs in their too-pale hands.

I glanced around the room. Everyone who wanted one had a mug and seemed comfortable enough. Rhiannon bit playfully at one of Preston's boots and I gave her a look. She raised her lip at me but settled down.

"It wasn't donations. It was a box from an estate sale. It was at the very bottom."

The book in question sat in the center of the coffee table. The teapot squatted in its cozy off to one side.

"And there's a key?" Cyrus asked.

"Oh yes," I said, digging it out of my front pocket, which is not an easy thing to do when you're sitting down and your jeans are as tight as mine are.

What can I say? Stefon likes them that way, and I don't mind showing off my curves.

I centered myself and lightly touched the leather cover of the book. It was embossed with strange arcane symbols I didn't recognize, and the lock looked as if it might bite. Again.

"That thing is seriously creepy," Tracy said. The teen was right.

"Sarah?" Uncle Cyrus asked, "Are you going to open it?"

"I guess I am," I replied. "But before I do, you should know...my mother came to me in a dream, and I think she was trying to tell me about this book. And the key."

Cyrus's eyes grew sharp, and Delta leaned forward in the kitchen chair she was perched on.

"Really? Did she say something?"

I shook my head, and the older witch subsided, taking a sip of her tea.

It would have been helpful to have more information, Mom. She didn't reply. Not even with an answering chime from her crystal ball on my bedroom altar.

Guess it was up to me. And maybe that was the message.

I sighed and looked back at the book. The key felt heavy in my fingers. I leaned forward slightly, letting the key hover right over the lock. I swore, as soon as the metal was within an inch of the lock, the book and the key began to hum. I could feel the vibration in my fingers.

"Oh, get on with it," Delta said.

I shoved the key home and turned it with a satisfying snick. The lock clunked open, releasing the metal bands holding the book closed. I removed the key and set it on the coffee table, giving Rhiannon and Preston a pointed glance. Both gnome and cat raised an eyebrow as if to say, *Who, us?* Like they had never gotten into any mischief with small objects before.

I kept my gaze steady and serious. Finally, Preston nodded, and Rhiannon blinked.

Good enough. I used my left hand to open the heavy cover and gasped.

Strange letters poured across the page as if alive, describing things I could not understand.

The teens both leaned forward, Stefon, too.

"What the heck kind of alphabet is that?" he asked.

"It's Theban," I replied. Just because I couldn't read it very well didn't mean I didn't recognize the glyphs and symbols.

Tracy wrinkled her nose. "Never heard of it."

"We haven't gotten that far in your studies yet, but trust me, you'll learn all about it."

"Can you read it?" Tabitha asked.

I shook my head. "I can make out a word or two. But the witch's alphabet was never something I was much good at, and like any language, you don't use it, you lose it."

Cyrus nodded in agreement and motioned with his hands for me to give him the book. I picked up the heavy tome and passed it over.

He flipped the heavy pages for a few moments as we all waited, sipping our tea, trying not to tap our feet. The fire crackled and the heavy paper made a whoosh sound each time he turned a page.

Finally, he looked up. "It's not a language I understand. I mean, I can read the Theban letters just fine, but can't make out what they're spelling."

"Is it a code?" Stefon asked. Cyrus raised an eyebrow and stroked his chin, looking back down at the book.

"You might be onto something. It very well could be a code."

I sat back heavily on the couch. "Why would someone go to the trouble of writing something in a locked book, in an alphabet almost no one can read, and then put it in a code?"

"And then," Tabitha said, "why in the heck would it end up in the bottom of a box in your shop?"

"Beware," Tabitha's father said.

What?

"You think the dead rats are connected to this?" I asked.

The vampire shrugged. "It can't be a coincidence now, can it?"

Well, most witches don't believe in coincidences in the first place. And was right. This was this was too much.

"Anyone good at cracking codes?" Tabitha's mother asked.

We all shook our heads and looked mournfully at the book in Cyrus's lap.

"I bet Ah Lam can," Tabitha said, eyes bright.

"Who's Angelica?" her mother asked.

Tabitha smiled and said "Only the coolest warlock ever."

Right as I said, "Cyrus's girlfriend."

Cyrus started to smile at Tabitha's words, but that changed into a scowl directed at me.

I waved my hands. "Right. Right. Not your girlfriend. I get it. But she's something, isn't she?"

This time he couldn't hide the smile.

"That she is," he said.

"We should also ask Mr. Hamamoto, too. He might know something," Tracy said.

That was a good idea. Tarot readers often studied all manner of strange things.

"Can I see the book?" Tabitha's mother asked.

As Cyrus moved to hand the leather monstrosity to the vampire, there was a clattering outside.

A clattering of hooves.

That could only mean one thing: a centaur had arrived. And the only time centaurs showed up at my house?

It wasn't for something good.

15

S erafina was on the street outside my cottage, black coat gleaming in the yellow of the streetlight. She pawed anxiously at the road as we all piled out of the house.

"Serafina," I said, "what's wrong?"

Her face looked grim.

"Trouble," she said. "At the casino. Hop on."

I shook my head. "Oh no. No way am I riding on your back all the way out to the casino."

While the Indian casino was a quick car trip down the highway, it was much farther—and much less comfortable—on horseback. Er. Centaurback. Do you know how jarring it is to ride a centaur at full gallop? And with my heavily endowed cleavage? There's not a sports bra in the world that can safely hold my girls in that situation.

"Fine," she said, "but you'll come?"

"Of course." I was honor bound to. Plus, I'm nosy.

"I'll drive," Stefon replied.

"So will we," said Tabitha's parents and Carol.

I turned to Tabitha and Tracy. "Don't you two have school in the morning?"

"It's Friday!" Tracy said.

Drat. One excuse to keep them out of danger gone.

Tabitha crossed her arms over her skinny chest. "Don't even think you're keeping us out of this."

I looked at Carol, and then at Tabitha's parents. They all just shrugged, giving me that look that just said, *Teenagers. What are you going to do?*

"All right," I said, "but if things look bad, you're leaving."

"Fine!" both girls said, stifling grins. I groaned.

If their parents said it was okay, who was I to argue?

Delta and Preston decided to ride with Stefon and me. Rhiannon chose to stay home, which was good. Speaking of which, I ran back in to the house, banked the fire, and closed the glass doors to keep it safe.

"Keep watch, Rhiannon!" I grabbed my purse and coat and ran out the door.

Soon enough, we were barreling down the highway.

"I wish she had said more," I muttered.

"You know centaurs," Delta replied from the back.

"Yeah," said Preston. "They don't like to share much."

"Which means this must be really bad," I said, looking out the window as we sped through our little town.

"If Serafina came to ask for our help? Sounds that way, babe. What do you need from me?"

The lights flashed over Stefon's face as we moved down the highway.

He was so beautiful, my boyfriend, and I was so lucky to have him.

"Just you being here is all I need. I won't really know anything else until we get there."

Stefon was already pulling off the highway into the big entryway to the Three Sisters Indian Casino. It wasn't a place I ever really went to except to hear a concert on occasion. The casino itself? I don't think I'd ever set foot in it.

He circled the drive, pulling into a spot near the casino doors.

"What now?" he asked.

"Good question." I peered into the parking lot, which was half full. Not surprising for a weeknight. On weekends the place was packed. And during the summer months too.

"We can't just barge in and ask why a centaur sent us here," Delta said.

"Does anyone see her?" Stefon asked. "Maybe I should drive near the edges. See where the parking lot leads out into the woods there?"

"Good idea," I said.

The rest of our strange little caravan had pulled up beside us. Stefon leaned out the window to explain what we were doing, then slowly made his way through the parking lot towards the small wild area at the edges.

And sure enough, I saw Serafina standing in the shadows.

"Stop here," I said, and scrambled out of the car. "Okay. We're here. Now what's the problem?"

The centaur was near tears, which stopped me in my tracks. I thought of Serafina as so stoic. The only strong emotion I'd ever felt from her before was anger. So to see her fighting to not cry gobsmacked me.

I moved forward, wanting to rush up and hug her, but I also didn't want to get kicked, punched, or bitten, so I forced myself to move slowly. I felt Stefon at my shoulder, and heard the soft voices of the others just behind us.

"Serafina?" I asked, much more gently this time. I can be sensitive if I need to.

"It's Máni."

The gentle centaur, pale as moonlight, Máni was the yin to Serafina's yang, he was the follower to her lead, and I'd a feeling he was also her confidant. There were other centaurs in their grove, of many shades and temperaments, but most had at least a tinge of Serafina's fierceness.

Máni must be quite special to have been singled out to be her closest friend.

"What's wrong with Máni?" I continued. "And why are we here?"

"Follow me," she said, then turned and walked into the mixed stand of pine and fir trees. It was hushed and beneath their fragrant canopy, muffling the sounds from the road and the casino.

I stumbled on a root, catching myself just as Stefon's strong hand gripped my shoulder, helping to stop me from stumbling further.

After the well-lit parking lot, it was very dim in the wooded area. I paused for a moment to let my eyes adjust, barely making out Serafina's dark, graceful bulk, weaving through the trees.

"Let's go," I murmured, stepping forward to follow again. Preston was muttering foul words, and being hushed by Delta Crabbit. I wondered what had upset the gnome, but we didn't have time to figure it out right now.

Serafina stopped just inside a small clearing, and I saw Máni. He was tethered to a tree by a silver chain, stamping his hooves and rolling his eyes in distress.

And at his feet was a woman, blond hair arrayed around her as she lay on the pine needle–strewn ground. She wore jeans, sneakers, and a heavy canvas work jacket.

I bent over her, holding a hand just above her nose and mouth to see if she was breathing as Stefon crouched across from me to check her neck pulse.

"That's Patricia!" Tracy exclaimed.

I looked up at the teen, her own blond hair a close match to the woman on the ground.

"You know her?"

Tracy nodded, Tabitha and Carol, too.

"She teaches pottery at the community center, and the community college outside of town." Tabitha replied. "She does special classes for youth. We love her!"

"All three of us have taken her classes," Carol said, stepping forward.

"Her pulse is even," Stefon said.

I looked up at Serafina. "What happened here?"

She shook her head but trotted closer. The little clearing was feeling crowded, what the two centaurs, Patricia on the ground, four human adults, and two teenagers.

My witch's hearing picked up the sound of what must be Tabitha's parents, moving through the woods. Hopefully they were looking for clues. Clues my human eyes would never see in this gloom.

"I'm not sure what happened," Serafina said. "I was at

our grove and felt Máni's call of distress. By the time I got here, the human was on the ground, and Máni was frantic. When I tried to get the story from him, he became so agitated, I tethered him in hopes that would calm him down. It did, but not enough."

Serafina looked uncomfortable, but whether that was at her friend's distress, or because she'd had to tether another centaur against his will, I couldn't tell.

"I think he's been sneaking out to meet this woman," Serafina said.

"Why would he have to sneak?" I asked.

Serafina set her mouth in a line and didn't reply.

Oookaaayy. Best to move on, I guessed.

"Carol?" I asked.

The blond witch stepped forward. Tracy stepped with her. Huh. The teen was responding as if I'd called her.

"Yes?" Carol asked.

"How's your empathy? Can you help Máni?"

"I can," Tracy said, before her mother could reply.

I looked from the teen to Carol. They looked so alike, standing there. I could see the witch Tracy would grow into. While she was still in the early stages of her training, we had worked on grounding, centering, and shielding. I knew she had a soft heart and had suspected that was linked to her being an empath.

I guess we'd find out.

"You can help him without getting drawn in?" Delta asked.

Good question.

Delta trying to stuff Preston back into the tote bag. The gnome was attempting to climb out. I guess Delta didn't want him to wander underneath a centaur's hoof, but the gnome was having none of it.

"If she can't, we're here to pull her out, aren't we?" Carol replied. Now that was good parenting. I made a note of it. Not that I intend to have children—at least no time soon—but as a magic teacher, I took the lesson to heart.

Sometimes we needed to let someone do their best but provide a safety net from a short distance. Cyrus had done it for me a hundred times, hadn't he?

Speaking of...

16

As soon as I thought of my honorary uncle, he glided into the clearing, silent as a vampire.

I gave him a *Where the heck have you been?* glance. He made a gesture that telegraphed, *We'll talk later.*

I wasn't happy about it but nodded back all the same.

Carol and Tracy stepped gingerly toward Máni. He snorted and rolled his eyes, backing away.

"Sshhhh," Tracy crooned, holding out both hands. "Shhhh. It's going to be okay. Try to breathe."

Máni whinnied, which was a strange noise coming from a human throat, let me tell you.

I crouched over Patricia again, and Stefon moved to make way for Uncle Cyrus.

He crouched as well, taking care to not get any dirt or pine needles on his clothing. Such a dandy. Sometimes I wished some of that rubbed off on me, but the reality is, I like T-shirts and jeans, and my sturdy black boots were much better suited for the conditions of Seashell Cove.

Like right now.

"What do you think?" I asked my uncle.

His eyes were soft—the gaze of a witch or warlock looking at energy patterns instead of solid things—and he passed them over Patricia's prone form.

"Something is draining her essence," he said.

"Her essence?" Tabitha's voice came from behind me, startling me. She was almost as quiet as her parents.

"Life force," I replied. "Soul. Prana. Mana. Core energy."

None of those words mapped the concept exactly, but together, they were close enough. The dark-haired teen nodded gravely. I could almost see her filing the information away.

Just then, her parents glided into the clearing, the smooth skin on their faces very slightly creased with concern. Dang vampires. They'd never worry about the aging process, would they? My sudden pang of jealousy was quickly replaced by the thought that, unless they were killed by a stake or something, they would have to watch their only daughter age and die.

Morbid much, Sarah?

"What is it?" Cyrus's voice was sharp, a rifle shot in the night.

"You have to see this. Please, follow me," said Tabitha's mother, Lisa.

We left Carol and Tabitha with Tracy and the centaurs. Delta and Preston kept watch over Patricia on the ground.

Cyrus, Stefon, and I followed the two vampires deeper into the tangle of trees.

What was my life coming to? First surround by

ghouls in a cemetery, then following vampires into a forest outside a casino.

Not the best life choices, but what's a witch to do? Especially being Justice. That was the biggest adjustment to that office, I think—that I all too often had to do things as my rational mind screamed "Stop!"

The two vampires stopped in front of a big pine tree. I bet Stefon couldn't even get his burly arms around the thing.

The tree was painted with blood, and five dead rats were arrayed like a star at the base of the tree.

The blood glowed, as if slightly phosphorescent. The letters spelled out that all too familiar word.

"Beware."

"Beware of what?" I asked, suddenly irritated. "I'm so sick of these riddles! Who the heck is leaving them?"

And why did I feel we'd been sent on a goose chase? I had a sudden pang of worry about Rhiannon, alone back at my house, and Tetris, and Angie, and all the others. I hoped they were okay. I hoped something bad wasn't happening to them while we were out here on the edge of town.

"What did you pick up?" Cyrus was asking.

"Traces of human scent. And faery."

"Like the sprites?" Stefon asked.

Tabitha's father gave a brief smile that was more like a grimace.

"Oh no," he said. "Much larger than that. Much taller, more purposeful, more cunning and brave."

"Seelie or Unseelie?" Cyrus asked.

"Does it matter? At the heart, all magical creatures are the same. We can all turn toward good or ill depending on what conditions we find ourselves in, can we not? Look at us." Tabitha's mother gestured to herself and her husband. "People think we are creatures of evil, but really? We're just trying to raise our child and make a life for ourselves, such as it is."

She had a point. I was going to learn a lot from Tabitha's parents, that was clear.

Cyrus took a turn around the tree and back again, scanning up and down. I could almost feel him sensing, and dropped into my center. I rooted my energy fields in the earth, and reached toward the sky, tasting the air.

It tasted of ocean and pine, blood, and...magic. Fae magic. Just as the vampires had said. There was an urgency about it, as if the message needed to be passed along quickly, almost brutally.

Because whatever these beings were warning us about?

It was big.

And coming fast.

17

It was a Saturday and Duncan was minding the store. I had gotten the teens set up in the back with the big tome and a Theban dictionary, figuring we might as well use their love of research and teach them the old classic witchy alphabet at the same time. And if they found out some information that was helpful? So much the better.

Meanwhile, I had to meet Delta down at Angie's. The witch was still intent on throwing a Samhain party. Or community gathering.

Whatever she was calling it, frankly, that was the last thing I wanted to do. But Delta insisted it would be good for the community, so I was playing along. At least for now.

I was tired as I walked down Main Street from my shop towards the Blueberry Café. It had been a late night. We finally got Máni calmed down and convinced him to leave Patricia in Cyrus and Carol's care.

Tracy's mother and my uncle had transported Patricia back to Carol's home where she had a guest bedroom and could keep an eye on her. Luckily, it wasn't spring, so Carol's business was in a lull. Oh, she always had work to do because she was a crackerjack accountant, but autumn was a slower time of year.

Cyrus said he would stay with Patricia as long as necessary. I had to trust the poor woman was in good hands. We still hadn't gotten the centaur to tell us exactly had happened, even after Tracy calmed him down. Serafina said she would work on him, but he needed to rest first.

I agreed. Clearly, something traumatic had happened. We weren't even sure why Patricia and Mani were at the casino. As usual, there were too many unanswered questions.

As I walked down the street, enjoying the autumn sun that peeked out between clouds, I wondered about our little town. It was such a special place and had always been weird. But it seemed to be getting stranger and stranger as years went by. Or maybe my parents and Uncle Cyrus had shielded me from some of what was really going on when I was younger.

Or it could have been that there was a change in the air. I couldn't tell. Yet another unanswered question.

"Mystery upon mystery," I muttered.

"Hey, Sarah." Tetris waved from across the street. I waved back. He motioned me over.

Looking both ways, I saw that traffic was light. So, I skirted across, not bothering to head towards the crosswalk.

"Any news?"

I shook my head. "Well, we got called out to the casino last night. The blond centaur? Mani? He was there, distraught, with the local pottery teacher splayed out on the ground. Cyrus and Carol are taking care of her. So that adds a wrinkle to all the things we haven't been able to figure out."

"Really? Patricia? She's the sweetest. Always helping out the local kids. Will she be okay, you think?"

I shrugged. We both looked at the sidewalk. To break the tension, I asked, "How about you? Any intel? Anyone strange come in the shop?"

The old punk rocker laughed.

"Someone strange is always coming in the shop."

I shared his laugh. It felt good to laugh.

"You have a point there, my friend."

"Here's the thing, though," he said. "I was thinking…"

My ears perked up. "About what?"

He leaned closer. "So, remember how the grig and the witch were using humans as go-betweens in the faery dust scandal?"

I nodded. That was an episode I was glad to put behind me. Stolen faery dust is no good for human beings, and I hope to never encounter a grig again. Mischievous little fae beings.

"Yeah, of course I remember."

After all, it only happened two months before.

"Well, what if something similar is happening here? What if some fae being or wizard or something else has a human envoy? And what if it is taking advantage of the ghouls to throw us off the scent?"

Dang.

"Well, Tetris, after last night, I think you're probably right. But the trouble is, how do we find out who it is and what do we do about it?"

He looked around. The street was still quiet, and no one was nearby.

"I have seen some new characters in town."

"Like who?"

"There's that larger white woman who wears several layers of coats and carries a lot of bags for one. She's new."

He was right. I had seen her around, though she hadn't come into the store yet.

"Who else?" I asked.

"There's also a man. Silver hair. Way too well dressed for this place. And I swear I saw a little kid."

I'd seen the man at Angie's, and with Roddy Devall. The kid, though? I hadn't seen a new kid.

"How little?"

"I mean, not little, little. Probably around thirteen. Like maybe Ash's age. And they were on their own. They looked kind of furtive, like they didn't want me to see them."

"Where was this?"

He gestured across the street.

"They were ducking down the alley behind Angie's, but by the time I turned the corner, they were gone."

I gazed toward the side street that led to the little parking lot behind the Blueberry Café, as if I could see the kid. As if they weren't long gone.

"You think they're in trouble?"

"Might be. I mean, it's not exactly tourist season, and I know all the kids in town because everyone comes into my shop."

That was true. Kids loved Ancient Treasures, what with all the dinosaur bones and fossils. But this still didn't get us any closer to answering the riddle of the dead rats or the book.

"Well, I'm heading to Angie's now to meet with Delta. I'll keep an eye out."

"I will too," Tetris said.

"Thanks, my friend. We've got a lot of smart people working on this. We'll figure it out."

He nodded and gave me a wave farewell.

But as I waited for a poky old Buick to pass so I could cross the street, I had to wonder.

Would we figure it out in time?

18

The meeting with Delta went on longer than I wanted. But at least I got a breakfast sandwich out of it.

I finally convinced the older witch that I thought her plans were great, and I would publicize the event if she wanted to. And that she should enlist help from Liam at The Historic Kelpie, along with Tabitha and Tracy. The teens were made for events like this. They would have things organized before I even boiled water for another cup of tea.

I just wasn't feeling the public Samhain. At least, not this year. There was too much to deal with, with the dead rats and the rest of this mystery.

Besides which, both my parents were still pinging me like crazy, disturbing my dreams and leaving messages in the shower steam on the mirror, which was a little disconcerting, considering I'm an adult and they haven't seen me naked in like, twenty years. Let's hope my opaque shower curtain was holding up its end of the bargain.

Also, last night, my mother's crystal ball kept humming from inside its box. It hadn't started chiming yet, though, so I figured I had a little more time to ignore it.

Besides, if my mom wanted to give me information about the book, she could spell that out in the shower steam, instead of last night's message, which was "Sarah, we love you. You drink too much tea."

My parents wanted attention that I wasn't sure how to give. And I wasn't sure what was up with that, either. I loved both my parents and would give anything to see them again.

Maybe that's what my problem with their sudden activity was. I was heartsore, thinking about them contacting me after death, when all I wanted was another day with them both alive.

I glanced at my watch. I really needed to get back to the store, but hoped Duncan could handle things for another half hour because I really needed to talk to Ash about that kid.

As I prepared to cross Main Street, I saw Roddy Devall across the street, haranguing someone. The person was seated on one of the public benches that dot Main and was huddled in on themselves.

I grimaced. I swore Roddy pressed his dark wash jeans to a crease. Who does that?

He had opened Devall Realty around eight months ago, selling properties and managing a lot of the vacation rentals around town. I hadn't run into him much, being all set on the housing front, but the few encounters I'd had didn't make me look too kindly upon the man. He was rather self-important and didn't seem willing to take time to fit into his new town before insisting everything bend his way.

I looked both ways again, then quickly crossed the street, heading towards him.

"You need to move!" he was shouting, narrow face shading from red to purple.

"I don't have to," said the person he was talking to. Their voice was firm, but also sounded as if they were using every bit of their courage to stand up to the bully that was Roddy Devall.

As I got closer, I saw that it was her, the woman Tetris had mentioned, with two layers of coats and three canvas tote bags around her feet. A sack of mixed seed peeked from one of the totes. She must have been feeding the birds, and while I understood the impulse, feeding birds in a tourist town was not the best idea.

Talk about nuisances, the gulls, corvids, and song-birds menaced many a tourist. At least the raptors kept their distance, but I could just imagine the terror in sunburnt faces should a bald eagle swoop in on a kid's fish sandwich, the way the gulls sometimes did.

I power walked toward Roddy and the woman.

"You're ruining this town!" he shouted, waving his slender, black merino sweater–clad arms.

I only know the sweater was merino because of Uncle Cyrus. Did I mention he's a dandy? Roddy Devall could only aspire to be as dapper as my honorary uncle.

I stepped up next to the woman and faced the shouting man.

"What's going on here?"

"This *person*,"—he practically spat the word, as if it was an insult—"is crowding our fair street."

He pointed a bony finger at the woman. Her skin was pale, with a slightly ruddy cast to her soft, round cheeks. Her pale, silver-shot hair looked clean, though was a bit of a bird's nest.

"I have just as much right to be on the sidewalk as anyone. These benches are public property."

"For the *paying* public. And you're scaring those away, aren't you? No tourists want to walk down Main Street looking at the likes of you. It makes the town look bad."

The woman straightened her back and glared at the Realtor. Good for her.

"Roddy, excuse me, please," I said. "First, it's October, which is not exactly tourist season. Second, she's right. The sidewalk is public property, and she has every right to be here, just like me or you."

"How can you say that Sarah Braxton? You're a small business owner, just like me. And she is a Bad. Element!"

I'd had enough.

"Roddy"—I pointed at his cashmere covered chest—"the only bad element in this situation right now is you. Why don't you go back to work and start drumming up business if that's what you're so concerned about? Leave this woman alone."

A shadow crossed his face, and for the first time, I thought he might be dangerous.

"You'd better watch your step, Sarah Braxton. I have my eye on you. Be aware."

The hairs stood up on the back of my neck.

"What did you just say to me?" I put every bit of witchy menace in my voice as I could.

His puce-colored face blanched, and he slowly backed away.

"You heard me," he muttered, then turned on his heel and practically ran down the sidewalk back to his office, leather soles smacking the concrete.

Who wears leather-soled shoes in constantly wet climate? Fools like Roddy Devall.

"Are you all right there?" I asked the woman.

Her face cracked wide with a grin. "You told him."

I laughed. "I guess I did. What's your name?"

"Tessa," she replied. "Tessa Connolly."

"Nice to meet you, Tessa. I'm Sarah."

"I gathered that," she said, jerking her head toward Roddy's back as he disappeared through the front door of his office.

I wondered if Mr. Roddy Jerkface knew anything about rats. Then had to remind myself that not liking someone was no reason to accuse them of lobbing random threats around town.

I turned back to the woman.

"Are you new here in town?" I asked.

"I am," she said, "going where the wind takes me."

"You have a place to stay?"

She smiled. "That I do. With some nice young kids on the edge of town. They rent a little house and let me park my trailer in their driveway. Use their shower, too."

"That's great," I said, making a note to look in on the young people and see if they needed any support or assistance with Tessa here.

But right now? Time was ticking.

"Well, I have to be going. You have a good day."

She raised her hand. "May the road rise to meet you. May the wind be at your back."

I swore the sidewalk beneath my feet tingled at the sound of the traditional Irish blessing.

I peered at Tessa, but she just smiled placidly back. More magic arrived to town. Or was it? She did have a bit of a fae twinkle in her eye.

Don't get ahead of yourself, Sarah. I glanced at my watch again, stifling a minor curse. I really needed to see Ash, but I also really needed to get back to the store.

I hurried down Main, to the side street where Ash's dad Jerry Hamamoto had a Tarot reading parlor that they lived behind.

It was a cute, neat little house on a quiet street with a sign out front advertising Jerry's skills. I hurried up the walkway between the shrubs that had brilliant flowers throughout the summer, but were now heading towards their winter guise.

Knocking on the door, I waited, tapping my foot impatiently. Soon enough, Ash opened the door.

"Miss Sarah, what are you doing here?"

"Ash? Who is it?" His father's voice carried from down the hall.

"It's just me, Jerry. Sarah. I need to talk to Ash for a moment."

I looked at the young, delicate-faced boy in front of me.

"All right, Ash?"

He nodded, leaning against the door jamb and twisting the old knob in one hand.

"Have you seen a new kid around town? About your age? Maybe he doesn't have a stable place to stay?"

His face fell. "Oh yeah. Him. He's not very nice, but I think it's because he's scared."

"Scared of what?"

Ash shrugged. "Not sure. But I caught him stealing from some of the stores. He made me promise not to tell. He's not homeless, though. He lives just outside town with his mom. In the trailer park, I think? Rides his bike in."

"Do you know his name?"

Ash shook his head. "He wouldn't tell me. Said he couldn't trust me yet. But I told him to come here if there was trouble."

Well, that wasn't good.

"Do you know which direction he lives in?" There were trailer parks to the north and south of Seashell Cove.

Ash pointed south. "Down that away."

There was an area just on the outskirts of town, set back from the main highway and Main Street. Along with the trailer park, there were a few of the older homes, well-weathered by the sea air. There were also a lot of trees and some old tree houses, built probably in the 1990s and now starting to decay. It was a perfect place for kids to hide. And get tetanus if they weren't careful.

"Thanks, Ash. If you see him again, would you text me? You have my number in your phone, right?"

He nodded, dark eyes looking grave. "I will, Miss Sarah." He started to shut the door. And then said "Um..."

"Yes."

"Should I tell my dad?"

I nodded. "I think you should, Ash. I think that would be a very good idea. The boy might need our help."

He filed that away, then said, "You have a good day."

"You, too."

Ash gave a little wave, then shut the door. I turned to head back to my shop, which needed attention.

And that other boy? He might need help from all of us. And sooner than I knew.

19

Stefon drove up the highway heading towards the edge of town to where Ash thought the boy lived. We planned to meet up with Cyrus and the teens later trying to see if they'd made any headway with the book. But for now, I had to follow all leads. Another rat had shown up one when none of us were looking, at the pottery shop down from Tetris's.

The owner saw it before he opened and had hurriedly cleaned things up without saying anything.

I didn't blame him. I only found out about it because apparently, he'd mentioned something to Angie, and she had sent me a text.

"This situation is so baffling," I said to Stefon. He glanced at me and returned his eyes to the road.

"More baffling than any other situation around this wacky town?"

"Well, you have a point there. But yeah, I mean, there's dead rats. There's warnings. There's ghouls. There's a book and a key. There's a new woman in town who may as well be homeless. There's a new boy in town who may or may not be in trouble."

I looked out at the ocean. An eagle soared beneath the gray clouds, looking for dinner.

"And much as I hate to speak ill of another member of the LGBTQ family, Roddy is being a jerk."

Stefon snorted. "What else is new? That guy."

"Right?" I said. "I've also seen him around with a stranger, who I can't get a proper read on. But so far, we've got a lot of possible suspects, but they're all pretty weak. And we have no real leads. Patricia still isn't well, though Carol said she'll question her as soon as she can stay awake longer than thirty minutes at a time."

I could practically feel my brow furrowing. "Like, any of these people could have something to do with the rats and the warnings. Any of these people could have something to do with the book or not. And what I can't see is how in the world these things are connected."

"Did you talk to the ghosts yet?"

"I haven't had time."

"You need to make time, babe."

He was right again, and chasing down this kid was likely a fool's errand. October nights on the Oregon coast came early, and it was already growing dark. We'd missed the sunset; it was just that strange, twilit gloaming time.

"I think it's just up ahead," Stefon said. The highway narrowed on this stretch. We'd already passed the ancient relic of a movie theater. It's two small screens showed one second-run film and one classic every week. The popcorn was terrible, but sometimes we went anyway and snuck our own food in.

"I think the trailer park is a couple turns past here."

We were headed south, which meant the place we were looking for would be on the left, away from the ocean. That's where the poorer people in town lived. The richer people lived either really close to the beach or at the top of the hill with the best views.

The rest of us lived in the no-view rows of more affordable housing. Stefon made more money than my parents or I ever would, so he had a view. Granted, it was only an apartment, but the view was pretty spectacular up there.

The only view my cottage had was a tiny slice of ocean from the backyard. If you craned your neck just right. But that's okay, I didn't need anything fancy, and could always visit Stefon's view whenever I wanted to.

Stefon put on his blinker, then turned left across the highway, guiding his SUV down a bumpy road filled with potholes. I was glad he was driving, and not me.

It was cool in green in here during summer, I bet, but this time of year? Things started looking a little grim. There were some small bungalows with peeling siding, some with neatly tended yards and others gone to seed.

You could see the people that still cared enough or had the resources enough to keep up their yards and houses and those who clearly did not. You can't blame anyone for poverty. At least not individuals. The larger systems at play, though? Those still needed to change.

Maybe someday my role of Justice would expand to include that, too. There were a lot of ways to help people, after all.

"Hey," I said to Stefon. "Do you think that we should lobby the city council to do more for people who might be fallen on hard times?"

He nodded. "I think it's a great idea. I've thought about it myself."

"You have?"

"Of course, babe. That's part of what being a knight means. Being of service."

I could barely make out the crumbling tree houses, farther back in the trees. It really was getting dark in here.

"Like what are you thinking? Pancake breakfasts?"

"Well, sure, pancake breakfasts on occasion. But I was thinking more a regular food pantry, maybe? Or some temporary low-rent apartments closer to town. I don't know." He shook his head. "Real estate. It's such a problem, isn't it?"

"It is," I agreed. And the obnoxious Roddy Devall wasn't helping.

"Let me put my mind to it," he said, as we came upon a row of trailers with vinyl siding. The kind people used to call mobile homes, except they weren't mobile at all. I mean, I guess they could be jacked up onto a semi truck and moved if they had to, but it wasn't as if they were on wheels or anything.

"This is an okay-looking a trailer park," I said. There were flower boxes, and even a small play area with one of those slide and swing set combos just past the row we were in front of.

"Yeah. It actually seems well maintained. I don't see any kids though. And no signs of them except the play area."

He was right. There were no bicycles or toys strewn about the way you would expect in a small enclave like this.

"I think there's something around the curve."

Stefon kept driving slowly down the ever bumpier road. And then we saw it. The less attractive mobile home park. The place where people really hard on their luck lived. There were garbage cans up front, overflowing as if the city hadn't bothered to pick them up, an old mattress dumped next to them.

I knew from a friend of mine in Portland that richer people often dumped their unwanted goods where poor or unhoused people lived. That way, they didn't have to pay dumping fees, and someone else would take the blame.

I wondered if that was what was happening here.

Just then, three kids, around Ash's age raced by on some dirt bikes, legs pumping, and hoodies flapping behind their skinny heads.

I bounced in my seat.

"There. I bet one of them is the kid we're looking for!

"Yeah, but which one? And what are we supposed to do? Flag them down?"

"We have to try," I said. "Chase after them!"

Stefon grunted but put the SUV in gear, speeding up while I leaned out the window, waving my arms, trying not to crack my head every time Stefon hit another pothole.

"Hey! Stop!"

The boys just pedaled faster, finally escaping in between two big trees.

"Dang. Lost them," I said, as Stefon rolled to a stop.

"But now we know where they live, or at least have more kids we can ask. We'll find them again, just you wait."

He backed the car into a dirt driveway and turned back towards the highway.

"What now?" I said, feeling kind of deflated. This whole trip felt like a waste of time, but no way was I chasing a bunch of kids through the woods when it was getting dark. Besides, I bet those kids knew the woods like the backs of their hands.

"Now I want a beer. And you need to talk to that uncle of yours about that creepy book."

He smiled as he said it, and I felt a rush of love for this man. Stefon wasn't a witch or a warlock. The only magic he had was whatever made him such a sought-after computer geek, and I guess being a knight gave him some sort of power, too.

But he loved me and loved my life and all my weird friends. He put up with all the magical scrapes I got into, helped me on cases when he could, and fed and loved me when he couldn't.

"I love you," I said.

"I know," he replied, with a face splitting grin. I punched his bicep at the cheesy *Star Wars* reference, then shook my hand out.

"Ouch. Why do you have to be so muscley?"

"You didn't complain about that the other night," he said. "And why do you have to be so weak?"

"You're so gonna get it next time we go on a run, big guy."

"Game on," he said.

20

On our way back into town, I saw Tessa walking on the edge of the highway with her tote bags, head down. She shuffled along on the ocean side of the road, opposite the highway from us. The streetlights and headlights flashed over her light hair and the canvas totes.

I swear, the woman was taking her life in her hands.

"Stefon! Stop!"

"What? I can't pull over here! What's happening?"

"Tessa! She's walking in the dark on the highway. She could get hurt."

My head whipped back, looking through the rear window of the SUV at the woman shuffling her way down the unsafe highway.

"Who?" Stefon asked.

"That woman I met on the street. Roddy Devall was harassing her. I think she knows something about the situation."

"Why do you think that?" he said, finally finding a

spot to pull over, and craning his neck to see if it was safe to cross the highway and turn around.

"I just have a sense. There's something about her."

"Babe. You have a sense about a lot of things. You're a witch."

"Yeah, so?"

"So, I'm just saying, sometimes other people are just ordinary folks trying to get through life. Not everything has significance and meaning. You know?"

I shook my head. "I don't believe that."

He looked at me, eyes intent.

"Babe, I'm not going to be able to make it across the highway. By the time we hit a light so I can make a safe U-turn, who knows where she'll be? Do you even know where she lives?"

I shook my head, looking past him at the stream of cars, the lights heading both directions.

"I don't exactly. She just said she lives back that way somewhere."

"I hate to say it, babe, but we're not going to be able to find her tonight."

I stared out into the darkness, listening to the crashing of the ocean.

"All right. Drive on."

We had appointments to make. Which reminded me, I needed to check in on Máni, but that was another thing we couldn't do in the dark. I wasn't about to go traipsing through the forest, seeking out the centaurs in anything other than daylight. I guess I could check in with Tabitha's parents. At least they'd be awake by now.

"Babe?" Stefon was waiting for me to make a decision.

"I guess head to The Kelpie. Cyrus said he got a room there to use as an office space."

And by office space, he meant a place to take meetings when he was forced to be in a place as poky as Seashell Cove.

My uncle likely wasn't sleeping there, because why would he? He'd recently bought a fancy house just outside Portland and could easily pop there to sleep. But I could see where having a temporary office in town would save whatever resource warlocks used to transport themselves.

Stefon put the car in gear and waited for a break in traffic.

"We can check in with Cyrus see what he and the teens have uncovered. And then we need to go talk to the ghosts."

"It's about time," Stefon said.

I gave him a look, but he just shook his head and drove. Stefon was never one to say *I told you so*. At least, not directly. I texted Cyrus as we headed down the highway. Both of us quiet, lost in our thoughts. Cyrus—for once in his life—texted me back, telling us that he was at The Kelpie, and the teens and Carol would meet us there. He would also let Liam know that we were coming.

My stomach growled, reminding me that I hadn't eaten enough that day. Good thing it was spaghetti dinner night at The Kelpie. See, witch's intuition works!

In short order we pulled into the parking lot behind the historic inn. Stefon shut off the engine, then turned to me. In the light from the dash, his eyes were like melting chocolate. And his lips looked pretty tasty, surrounded by the soft, dark, curls of his beard. Yeah. I was definitely hungry.

"Hey," he said softly.

"Hey yourself," I replied. And he leaned across, and I leaned forward, and we kissed. Just a short, sweet one. He wrapped his arms around me and just held me close for a moment.

"How'd you know I needed that?" I finally said.

"Babe," he said as he pulled away. "I know you, and I love you."

Swoon. "Thanks for being so good to me."

"You make it easy. Now, let's go talk to some ghosts."

As soon as we opened the car doors and stepped out into the small parking lot, the smell hit me.

"Stefon?" My voice quavered, which was disconcerting. My voice never quavered.

He stopped mid-step and turned toward me, leaning close.

"What's wrong?"

I shook my head. "Not sure. But something doesn't smell right."

He sniffed the air, and wrinkled his broad nose, grimacing. "Rancid."

"It's coming from over there." I pointed toward the garden at the rear of The Kelpie. Calling it a garden was an understatement. I mean, sure there were plants, but there were also sculptures, a chicken carnival, towering trees, a boat being attacked by a fake shark, and whatever else struck Liam's fancy.

The garden during the day was a pleasant, amusing jaunt through wonderland.

The garden at night?

Let's just say I didn't want to know what was lurking there.

"We need to check it out," Stefon whispered. "Should we call for backup?"

"Let's see if anything's there, first. Might just be another dead rat."

We both knew I was lying. The smell was too strong to be a single, drained rat. As a matter of fact, it smelled an awful lot like a ghoul.

"Ssss-aaaaaiiirrrr-uhhhh."

"Well, that's not creepy," Stefon said.

"Hecate help me," I prayed. I mean, I don't pray often, but sometimes its a better option than peeing my jeans.

"We neeeed to talk to yoooouuuuu."

"Ugh. What should we do?"

The stench increased. Microwaved fish, dirt, and decay. Nice.

"Your call, babe. But I think we should text Liam."

I inhaled, then gagged, waving my hands to try and clear the air.

"Do it," I choked out. My body trembled with fear. Then I grew angry. Who were these ghouls to mess with my mind this way? To lie in wait and scare me like this?

I was a witch, dammit. And I was Justice around these parts. No ghoul was going to manipulate me, or cow me into submission.

I willed my feet to step toward the back of the historic inn, to where who knows how many ghouls waited in the shadows.

"Sarah! Wait!" Stefon wasn't trying to be quiet anymore. He fell into step beside me. "What the heck, Sarah?"

I didn't reply. Yes, walking back here alone, even for a moment, was foolish. But I was done with people—whoever or whatever they were—threatening my town.

And we still didn't know what happened with Patricia and the centaurs. We didn't know what was happening with the book, or the rats, or the ghouls.

Samhain was coming, I missed my mom and dad, and just wanted to enjoy the holiday in peace.

"I'm ending this," I said. "Now."

21

I stood at the edge of the parking lot, between the courtyard and the garden that ran the entire back half of the inn.

The back garden was mostly in darkness with only a few lights glowing beneath the tall trees and highlighting a few of the strange sculptures. One light reflected off the base of the rowboat making the the massive shark head rising from the earth all the more menacing, while the poor sailor just trying to get home was in shadow.

I really didn't feel like setting foot in there.

"Saaairruhh."

The voice hissed from behind one of the trees.

"Slow down, babe," Stefan said, though I wasn't exactly barreling toward the garden, eager to shake a ghoul's undead hand.

But I slowed down anyway. The last thing I needed was to twist my ankle. I'd had plenty of that nonsense a couple of months ago.

I skirted the small courtyard outside the Kelpie

dining room and headed into the shadowy garden behind. The lighting back here really was barely adequate. I bet the opossums, raccoons, and other creatures of the night appreciated it. Even as my eyes adjusted to the darkness, I followed my nose, really wishing I had a scented handkerchief to hold over my face.

Note to self, start packing a menthol stick in my jeans.

"Sarah!" Liam's voice called out, and the light above the back door to the kitchen flicked on. "Why are you out in the garden? What's wrong?"

"Ghouls!" Stefon shouted back.

I heard a stifled curse from Liam followed by the murmuring of other voices. And then, *pop* out of nowhere, Uncle Cyrus was at my side, his frankincense smell adding an undernote to the microwaved fish, graveyard dirt, and ocean air smells. I jerked back, slapping my hands against my chest.

"Dang it, Cyrus! It's what, five yards from the kitchen door? You couldn't just walk it?"

My uncle shrugged one cashmere-covered shoulder. "I wasn't certain how imminent the danger was. What's happening?"

"Ghouls."

"I can smell that," he said, voice dry. "But why are they here?"

"Well, we haven't found that out yet, have we? We haven't actually been sitting around drinking cups of tea and having a chat back here."

The lead ghoul from the cemetery stepped forward. Next to him was the sly ghoul, and a third I didn't recognize. But all ghouls look pretty much the same. Once your flesh is rotting, your features become a lot less distinct.

"What do you want?" I asked. Not the most polite greeting, but I was in no mood.

"We seek your help," said the lead ghoul.

"Oh, *now* you seek my help. How about when we needed *your* help? Hmm? How about that? How about when we needed our questions answered?" I leaned toward the ghoul as Stefan and Cyrus both held me back with a hand on each of my shoulders. I poked my finger in the general vicinity of the tattered clothing covering its chest. "Hmm. How about that? I'm sick of you ghouls. I'm sick of dead rats, and warnings, and the smell of microwaved fish!"

"We are sssoorry, Ssaarah."

"Sorry? Sorry for what?"

The lead ghoul looked at the ground.

"For frightening you the other night. We were following instructionsss, and firssst, it seemed like a lark. But then we grew frenzied, drunk on the power of your fear. And then…"

"And then what?" Stefon growled, voice filled with menace.

The three ghouls leaned away, as if trying to decide whether Stefon was a threat.

The lead ghoul looked at me with his glowing, undead eyes. "And then one of our own wasss murdered, and we woke up sssomehow."

"You can murder a ghoul?" That was Tracy's voice, coming from near the building. Great. the teens were getting an education I hadn't intended.

"They rent her limb from limb and scattered her

bones around the cemetery as a warning. And they painted the word *Beware* on a headstone."

I turned to Cyrus. "This is not good."

He shook his head. The porch light gleamed off the dark, bald dome of his head, and his face looked pensive.

"No. It is not. I fear we may have to get the council involved once more."

I groaned. Involving the council was never high on my list of things to do. They were a bunch of old, fuddy-duddy stick-in-the-muds if you ask me. But I had to admit that Cyrus was right: sometimes, when push came to shove, the council were the only recourse.

"And what do you mean by you 'woke up somehow'?" Tabitha asked.

Good question. I had missed that part.

The lead ghoul shook its head, teeth clattering in a truly disturbing way.

"It was as if we were under a compulsion. And there were new ghouls among us, ghouls we had not seen before. They whipped us up. Encouraged us."

"Made things worse," the third, shyer ghoul said.

"Can you help us, Sssarah?" the lead ghoul asked again.

"Help you how, exactly?" I put my hands on my hips and stared from ghoul to ghoul. I swear, this job of mine is the weirdest. The ghouls were trying to gain my sympathy, but hadn't succeeded.

Yet.

"Find out who did thisss and kill them?" asked the sly one.

"Slow your roll there, dead person," I said. "It's not my job to go around killing people."

"Do you even know who these people are so we can find them?" Stefon asked, bringing the voice of reason to the conversation. "I mean, you were helping them, right, whether you were compelled to or not?"

Yeah. That whole "following instructions" thing bugged me. Who the heck was compelling ghouls to do their bidding?

The lead ghoul shook his head mournfully.

"All I know isss they had great power. Power to create and dessstroy. And they sssmelled funny."

Huh. Coming from a ghoul, "smells funny" was quite the dig, but it could actually be our first piece of useful information.

"Smelled funny, how?" Tabitha asked. The teens, Liam, Delta, and Carol had all moved closer to our little circle.

"There were two of them. And we could not tell if they were human, magic, fae, or sssomething elssse. Their ssscent was...scrambled. Dissstorted. Unclear."

I thought quickly, scanning through the information we had already gathered.

We'd gotten mixed reports of things that seemed fae, things that seemed magic, and things that seemed human, but I had been thinking it was three separate beings. Knowing it was two made me all the more confused.

"What type of beings have such muddled energy signatures?" I mused out loud.

"Could be changelings," Cyrus said, "but I'm not sure."

"But you'll help usss?" The lead ghoul actually sounded hopeful.

I looked into its undead eyes.

"I'll do my best. But no more dead rats, okay?"

"A ghoul must feed, but we shall try to keep our leavings from these creatures' hands."

"Fair enough," I said, then turned to the ragtag group of friends standing behind me.

"Guess our meeting now includes this discussion."

"And we ssshall be on our way," said the lead ghoul. "Being far from the cemetery isss not good for ghoulsss."

Hmm, more information to file away. Learn something new every day.

"Before you go," I asked, "are the unfamiliar ghouls still bothering you?"

All three shook their heads this time. The shy ghoul's head almost turned 360 degrees. I might wish for that kind of flexibility, but really? Yuck.

"They left after you did and went streaming down the hill."

Great. So not only did we have dead rats to contend with, and strange, maybe fae, maybe human, maybe magic beings killing dead things, there were rogue ghouls roaming who knows where?

For once in my life, I had nothing to say about any of it. Confusion roiled inside my skull.

The ghouls faded into the shadows as we watched.

I turned toward Liam. The innkeeper was literally wringing his hands. I hadn't seen him so upset since a dead body was found in this garden.

"Liam," I said, "do you think you can make us all a pot of tea?"

"Yes, yes, I'll do that. Tea. Tea. I'll do that," he stammered, nodding his head so hard I thought it might shake off. But as I suspected, he was happy to have something to do. He raced back through the garden toward the kitchen door, slamming the screen door behind him.

I rubbed between my eyebrows where a headache was rapidly forming.

"All right, everyone, back inside. Seems like we have a lot to discuss."

And as usual, more questions than answers.

I hoped the ghosts were around to help.

22

The ghosts had proved elusive the night before, despite our best efforts to round them up. So, Cyrus and I had decided a visit to the centaurs was in order.

After a restless night, I piloted my roomy new turquoise hybrid along the highway, heading away from the ocean and into the woods. Cyrus was with me, the giant tome of a book open on his lap.

"Any luck?" I asked. "Have you gotten any further with the translation?"

"It's very strange," he said. "I've never seen anything like it. Not in all my years of investigation and working with the council. I can make out a word or phrase here and there, and the teens did a pretty good job of pointing towards the code. But we haven't quite cracked it yet."

"I don't understand," I said. "If you can read words or phrases, doesn't that mean you cracked the code?"

"You'd think so."

I navigated the twists and turns of the highway as

Cyrus worked out how to explain it. I knew that feeling all too well.

"There seems to be some weird double cipher. And if it wasn't sitting here in my lap, I wouldn't have believed such a thing was possible."

I headed away from the ocean, towards the centaur's sacred grove, looking for landmarks along the way. And by landmarks, I mean particular trees and rocks. Cyrus and I had been here once before, uninvited, and let me tell you, that was an unsettling and frightening experience.

At least this time the centaurs expected us.

I wound my way onto one of the tributary roads that fed deeper into the woods. It was darker beneath the heavy canopy of Douglas firs. I switched on my lights.

Finally, we reached the spot I remembered, and I pulled into a little offcut and parked the car.

As I unbuckled my seatbelt, Uncle Cyrus wrapped the book in a piece of canvas, then waved his fingers over it in a series of arcane shapes that I only assumed would cloak the book from those who didn't already know it was there. He then wrestled it beneath the front seat.

"Ready?" I asked.

"Ready."

And then off we went, traipsing through the woods, walking down a deer path. Me, in my sturdy black hiking boots, and Cyrus as usual in his completely impractical Italian leather shoes. The man never got a speck on him, which frustrated the heck out of me and meant he had enough magic to waste to keep himself looking neatly pressed and clean at all times.

Not me.

I saw Serafina up ahead, arms crossed over her narrow chest. She did not look happy. Not that she ever did, at least, not in my presence. But today she looked downright concerned and actively angry.

She lifted a hand in greeting and immediately turned and trotted back off into the groove. I guess that was the only hello we were going to get.

I hurried behind her as she led us through the main grove into another copse of trees.

"Where is she taking us?" I muttered to my boots. Cyrus was silent. Soon enough, I saw there was a series of buildings with rooftops and open sides. Dotted among them were a few that were enclosed on three sides. Two of these had steel fire pits near the front with chimneys funneling the smoke high up into the trees.

I hoped the chimneys had good grates on top, otherwise they risked setting the whole forest ablaze, which was the last thing we needed. Wildfires were increasingly a concern around these parts, thanks to all the greedy corporations who didn't give a good gosh darn about climate change.

But I guess the centaurs had lived here longer than I had and knew better. Right?

Serafina's black horse rump disappeared into the building on the right, one of the ones with a fire.

I paused in the entryway, allowing my eyes to adjust, and saw Máni, his white coat looking dull. He was lying down on the floor, four legs tucked beneath him, head bowed, arms wrapped around himself, with a striped blanket over his shoulders.

He looked up when we entered. His eyes had purple shadows beneath them. He looked gaunt, as if the life had been sucked out of him overnight. Kind of like one of our ratty friends.

I exhaled slowly, and then moved towards him.

"Máni," I said quietly, crouching down next to the centaur. He said nothing.

I looked up at Serafina, who nodded. Taking that as permission to do whatever felt right, I reached a hand toward the blond centaur, and gently laid it on the blanket on top of his shoulder. He was trembling.

"Máni, can you tell us what happened, so we can try to help you?"

He shook his head at first, then took in a long shuddering breath.

"They blasted me. And then her. They started to drain her, and I tried to stop them. She is my friend. I couldn't stop them."

"You did stop them, Máni. She's alive, isn't she? And getting better?" Serafina's voice was harsh as a crow's. I could feel the anguish radiating off her at seeing one of her people so distressed. "You stopped them from killing her."

"Yes, but I didn't stop them from draining her life force, did I?" His voice sounded tight, as if he had been screaming. Perhaps he had.

Cyrus came to stand beside us.

"But you stopped them before they could take it all," Cyrus said. His voice was soft, but firm. "What can you tell us about them?"

Máni looked up at my uncle with anguished eyes.

"There were three of them," Máni said. "At least, I think so. One human, one fae, and one smaller being that

I'd never seen the likes of before. It was almost as if it was a combination of the two."

I glanced Cyrus, who nodded gravely.

"What did they look like?" I asked.

"It was all very confused, and I did not see much. There was a tall, fae figure, a much smaller, quicker creature, and a third person. I think the third person was human. The fae figure seemed in charge."

"Could you get any information about the human?" I asked.

Máni looked at me, eyes sorrowful.

"The third person was not really there. I saw them, then they were gone." He pondered for a moment, eyes gazing toward the fire at the front of the dark structure. "But I think..."

"Yes?"

"I remember something about shopping."

"Shopping?" Cyrus asked.

Máni shook his head again. "I don't know. But I think there were bags leaning up against one of the trees."

I choked. Tessa? Was it Tessa and her bags? I couldn't believe it. Tessa was so nice. She seems so innocuous. I had wanted to help her.

I was filled with anger and horror.

"What do you know?" Serafina asked, studying my face like I was a bug.

"I've met someone who carries a lot of bags," I temporized.

"Can you bring us to this person?"

No no no. This was very bad.

"Serafina, I don't think..."

"You. Do. Not. Get to decide." Serafina's mouth was

set in a straight line, her face severe. "This person has harmed one of ours and one of his friends. It is up to us now. You lead us to their lair."

There was one problem with that. I didn't exactly know where Tessa lived.

Or if had been her at the casino at all.

23

After dropping Cyrus back at the hotel, I needed to clear my head. So, I called Stefon, and he met me at the beach for a jog. We tried to get out to run a couple times a week, and it was the best thing for my mental health ever. We jogged past what I called the fallen giants. These were massive tree trunks with huge, gnarled and grasping roots laid out along the sand next to driftwood piled into strange pyramidal sculptures by intrepid artists.

I huffed out a breath and ran. Two. Three. Four. I exhaled again with another gust, my lungs naturally filling up as I ran. That was the secret that my running teacher showed me years ago: do a big gusty exhalation every four steps and the lungs took care of the rest. It was the thing that finally got me converted to running. Before that, I'd always found it awkward and exhausting. Now, it was exhilarating.

When I ran, I felt free, even with my breasts strapped within an inch of their lives.

Great clouds gathered over the ocean and gulls squawked and shouted at each other.

There were a few people scattered here and there. Stefon and I were the only two runners. There were no kites in the sky. No screaming children. Just the two of us, the wild Pacific Ocean, and the sounds of my breath and our feet smacking on the sand.

Stefon pulled up next to me. We paced each other for a while, slowing down to enjoy each other's company.

"Any ideas yet?" he asked.

I shook my head. "The more information we get, the more tangled this whole situation becomes. I still don't believe Tessa would hurt anybody. I've got a feeling there's someone out there putting a whammy on folks."

"A whammy?" Stefon smirked, but didn't stop running.

"You know. Like, a compulsion. Controlling them somehow."

We jogged on, zagging past the small, clear blobs of jellyfish dotting the sand.

"How about Patricia? Has she remembered anything?"

I grimaced. I really needed to go visit the woman. She was still convalescing in Carol's spare bedroom.

"By all accounts she doesn't remember much. A friend of hers works at the casino. She'd gone to visit her, and then arranged to meet Máni in that copse of trees afterward. She remembers a struggle and a flash of light, but not much more."

"Are she and the centaur lovers or something?"

I lifted my hands and dropped them again in a *Your guess is as good as mine* gesture, and kept jogging.

"I didn't ask. And I kind of don't want to know. I mean, a human and a centaur? How would that even work?"

Some things were better off left to the imagination. Or not.

"At any rate, they're certainly friends. Máni says they're working on a project together. He had just caught sight of Patricia and waved her over. She was headed to the spot where the parking lot meets the woods, and there was this whooshing sound, a terrible stink, and a flash of light that blinded Máni temporarily. When his eyes cleared, she was on the ground. And all she remembers is about the same. The sound, the smell, the flash of light, and then waking up in Carol's room with a massive headache."

"Was it the ghouls? I mean, they stink."

"Maybe. But Máni didn't mention any ghouls. There were more rats, though."

We were coming to the end of our usual course, so I angled my steps off the damp sand, toward the dry stretch leading to the steep stairs that would take us to the top of the cliff.

"Patricia also said there was the scent of roses. And Máni smelled that too."

Running on the soft, dry sand became too difficult to do while talking, we continued our jog in silence for a while. Then it was the endless climb up the flight of stairs to the parking lot.

I was winded by the time we reached the top, and did my usual turn to look at the view. It was spectacular, as always. I never tired of the Pacific Ocean, no matter what the season.

"Dinner at my place?" Stefon asked.

"I'd love to, but I think I need to meet with Cyrus again and work on all of this."

"Want some moral support?"

I smiled at my handsome geek of a boyfriend.

"You know I'd love it. And Cyrus may not always act like it, but he appreciates your company, too."

"All right, then."

He drew me in for a big, long, sweaty kiss, then we parted.

"I'll shower and change. Meet you at Costa's?" he said. Cyrus's favorite place in town.

"Sounds good." I buckled myself into my own car and sat for a while looking out at the ocean, at the rolling waves and the gulls. I'm not sure why I sat there. I guess I was hoping the view would jog my brain, dislodging some clue I had missed. Around the cliff tops, swallows chased each other, arcing happily through the sky.

The run had done me good. I felt more balanced and centered, but I was no closer to cracking this case than I had been before.

Before I turned the car on I caught a flash of sandy-blond, silvery hair. It was Tessa with her many coats and bags.

I got out of the car and waved, shouting her name.

When she saw me, she looked scared. Not so friendly anymore. She scurried away down the highway back towards town.

"Dang it!"

What could I do, but follow?

24

"Tessa!" I called again, then beeped my car shut and raced across the parking lot, grateful I was in running togs and my barefoot-style shoes. I had to be much quicker than an older woman laden down with tote bags, right?

But by the time I cleared the parking lot and crossed the busy highway to Main, she was gone.

I slowed down and scanned the rows of shops to my left, then to my right. There was the beloved T-Rex statue outside of Tetris's shop. There was the pottery store. Angie's bakery. Roddy's realty shop.

And there was the edge of a tote bag, swinging its way through the door to the ice cream parlor.

"Gotcha," I muttered, then loped down the street toward Rainbow Sprinkles. Peering through the window, past the cardboard jack o'lanterns, black scaredy cats, and signs announcing "freshly made waffle cones!" and "spooky new flavors!" I saw Tessa.

She was waiting behind a parent and two kiddos, peering furtively over her shoulder.

Her eyes widened when she saw me looking back, head swiveling around the shop as if she was looking for another exit.

I flung open the door, then slowed my roll, smiling and entering as if I had nothing more on my mind than whether or not a black sesame and green tea ice cream would make a good combo.

When I stepped up beside Tessa, she backed away. I stepped again. She backed again. We repeated this process three times until she sat with an *oof!* onto one of the spindly chairs at a little glass-topped table. I tried to never sit in those chairs.

As far as I could tell, they were designed for size fourteen butts and under. I mean, I wasn't heavy enough to break one, but that didn't mean they were comfortable.

I sat across from her, making sure the kids, their parent, and the ice cream scooping specialist were still occupied.

"Is there a reason you're running from me today?"

Her eyes widened again. They were a soft, sea-foam green. I didn't even know eyes came in that color.

"You're a witch," she blurted out.

At normal volume. Great.

I jerked my head back toward the counter. The kids were engrossed in their cones, and the parent was paying. If anyone had heard Tessa's little outburst, they weren't letting on.

"Yes. I am. What does that have to do with anything?"

She sighed, and looked out the window toward Main,

though there wasn't much to see other than gray sky and some store banners flapping in the October ocean breeze.

"You're also a Justice."

"You've been asking about me."

Tessa looked back at me, eyes serious. "Of course, I have. Someone walks up to help me, brimming with magical power, when I'm facing down a foe, I ask some questions."

The little family left the shop. The clerk was eyeing us now. I nodded and smiled, then gave a little *Give us a minute* wave. He turned and started cleaning up the prep space, rinsing out scoops and refilling napkins.

"We should order," I said. "Can I buy you something? Coffee? Ice cream?"

I wanted her to stay put until I got some answers. If I confronted her right away, she'd probably bolt, and I'd never see her again.

She nodded. "Both, please. Large. Whatever flavors look good. In a cup."

I rose, patting my running leggings for the secret pocket that held my keys, ID, and credit card.

"And you won't leave?"

She settled back in her chair and began arranging her tote bags. "I won't leave."

I placed our order, deciding to test out the green tea and black sesame combo, paid, and sat back down with Tessa's coffee and a mint tea for myself. I needed some calming down. I also needed a strategy for dealing with Tessa.

Was she just a regular itinerant person with a little extra psychic oomph? Was she a witch, a warlock, or something else, and well-cloaked from prying psychic eyes?

Or did she have one of the types of neurodivergence that lent itself to flashes of clear sight? That was a lot more common than people thought.

For all I knew, there was a magical object in one of those bags that set off psychic interference against the likes of me.

Or this case could just be making me more paranoid than usual.

We sipped our drinks in silence for a moment, blowing across the hot surfaces, and making polite noises about warm drinks on cool days.

The clerk brought out our ice creams in old-fashioned glass dishes. Setting down spoons and napkins, he asked, "Anything else I can get you?"

"We're good, thanks," I replied. Once he was safely back behind the counter, I leaned forward across the table. Tessa leaned back again.

She really didn't like me inside her energy field.

"How did you know I was magic?" I asked.

"You practically scream it out, just walking down the street. Didn't you know?"

I shook my head.

"I didn't."

No one had mentioned it before, and I had pretty darn good shields myself, so she must be really sensitive.

We both decided it was time to try the ice cream.

Oh, heck yeah. The black sesame was amazingly rich and blended nicely with the green tea. I was oh so getting this combo again.

"Have you been psychic all your life?" I asked. A lot of

psychics were that way from age five or six, which made childhood a challenge. You had to learn to not say out loud what you were seeing, hearing, or otherwise sensing. Other people? A trauma brought on dormant skills.

She took another spoonful of ice cream—hers was cherry chocolate—and nodded thoughtfully.

"It made my life hell. My parents hated it. Tried to beat it out of me. Took me to a preacher who made me kneel for hours at a time, while he shouted 'the devil' out of my body."

I set my spoon down, stomach clenching.

"That sounds terrible." The words were inadequate, but what can you do?

Tessa nodded and took another sip of coffee. "It really was. I lied and told the preacher and my parents that God had taken away my powers. I got really good at masking what I sensed from that point on. Trouble was, as I got older, my particular combination of clairvoyance and clairsentience made it hard to work around a lot of people, or to go to school, even. So here I am."

She swept her hand up and down her many-coated body and the tote bags at her feet.

"You never got training?"

"Didn't know it was a thing until it felt too late."

I picked up my spoon. "It's never too late. A lot of people in this town would be willing to help you if you wanted."

A wistful look passed over Tessa's face. It made me sad. My want-to-be-a-good-person parts wanted to take her under my wing and give her the help everyone deserved.

But the Justice in me still didn't know how much I

could trust her. Besides, I had a hunch. Nothing clear, but a hunch nonetheless.

"So," I asked. "What do you know about the dead rats? And the woman in the casino parking lot? I think you were there that night, weren't you? Who are you protecting?"

She grew pale, and almost spit out her coffee, devolving into hacking coughs, a napkin pressed against her mouth. I slid a water glass across the table. Tessa nodded, and took a grateful sip, eyes watering and still wary.

Tessa was frightened.

"How did you know I was protecting someone?" she whispered.

"You wouldn't have run from me to protect yourself. I saw how calm you were with Roddy. You wouldn't be scared of one witch asking questions. I think you ran today because you don't want to get someone else in trouble."

We stared at each other for a few long moments. I still wasn't convinced she was a threat. At least, not the main threat. She had to be covering for someone else.

I took another bite of my ice cream, hoping she would answer if I gave her more time. Then my phone buzzed in the holster pocket of my running leggings, reminding me I was supposed to be showered and en route to dinner ten minutes ago.

Darn it.

I quickly texted Stefon that I'd be twenty minutes late and to make nice with Uncle Cyrus. Then I texted Cyrus to basically say the same.

"I have to go soon, but before I do, I want you to tell me what you know."

Tessa looked like she was fighting tears, which made me feel worse about leaving in the middle of this.

I took a risk and reached out, laying a hand on her coat sleeve.

"Look, I know you're involved in this somehow, but whatever it is, we can work on it together."

I could tell she didn't believe me, and frankly, I didn't blame her.

"Tessa, you're not alone, okay? Not if you don't want to be."

"It's Zach," she whispered. "He's in some kind of trouble but won't tell me what it is. I tried to follow him that night, at the casino, but I was blinded by a white flash and when I woke up later, you were all there, so I hid. And that Roddy has been bothering him, too, just like he was bothering me."

"Zach?"

"He's just a boy, Sarah. Please don't hurt him."

My mouth was suddenly dry. I oh so did not want to go up against a kid. Even a kid who may just have dangerous powers.

"Do you know what he's done?"

She shook her head. "No. I just know there's been trouble. And his poor mother works two jobs...she's just not around much. I offered to talk things through with him one time, but he just got on that bike of his and raced away."

"All right. Like I said, we'll figure this out. Did you see anything else? Before the flash?"

She shook her head. I thought she was telling the

truth, but if she was a powerful enough psychic, she could be hiding things from me, too.

I glanced at my watch and stifled a curse. "I've got to go now. But if you hear or see anything, please let me know."

I raced back to the parking lot and my car, but what was I headed to, besides dinner?

And what was coming next?

25

I rushed into Costas, hair wet and in clean jeans, boots, a long sleeve T-shirt, and my trusty green jacket. Oh, I'd also donned a beautiful navy and green sweater that Stefon had gifted me for no particular reason other than he's nice like that.

I scanned Seashell Cove's only semi-fancy restaurant and sure enough, at our usual booth table by the giant plateglass windows looking out at the stormy ocean were Cyrus and Stefon, two Black men in a seventy-percent-white town.

They couldn't have been less alike. Stefon was burly and bearded, with a full head of curly natural hair and a tendency towards jeans and geeky T-shirts. Though he also had a nice sweater on over what I was sure was some D&D or medieval themed T-shirt. Whereas Uncle Cyrus with his shaved bald head and no facial hair was dressed as if he was heading to Paris at any moment.

Which was often the case, frankly, since warlocks can

pop wherever they want, whenever they want, like they have their own gosh-darn transporter.

Cyrus could have been in Paris this morning for all I knew. Stefon's face lit up when he saw me, and my heart went a little squishy inside. Yeah. He was a keeper. I don't know why I resisted admitting that for so long.

I waved at the hostess and pointed to their booth. She nodded and waved me, on never stopping talking on the phone.

I skirted my way through the tables of the half-empty restaurant. Stefon scooched over in the booth. He was halfway through some pale beer, and Uncle Cyrus was working on what had to be a glass of Cabernet, since that was his favorite wine.

"I ordered you a Pinot Grigio," Stefon said. He gave me a peck on the cheek. True to his word, a waiter approached with a glass of pale wine made of Oregon grapes.

He also took our food order. Usually, I ordered fish and vegetables here, because, duh. The fish here was expensive and really, really good.

But tonight? I wanted a hamburger and fries. Stefon ordered the same, and Cyrus got his usual steak and steamed vegetables.

"What happened?" Stefon asked, once the waiter walked away. "I thought you were heading straight home."

"I was, and then I saw Tessa."

"Tessa?" Cyrus asked.

"She's the not-quite-homeless person that Roddy Devall was harassing on the street the other day. We saw her walking on the highway last night, and I wanted to talk to her. She carries a lot of bags. I have a feeling she knows more than she's letting on, so I chased her down. And turns out sure enough, she's psychic."

"So?" Stefan said. "Aren't a lot of people? And did you ask her if she was at the casino?"

"Yes, a lot of people are psychic, but she's something special. I asked her about the rats and the centaur, and she looked terrified. Turns out she was at the casino that night but got blinded by the same flash that caught Máni." I looked at Stefon. "And she's trying to protect the boy. She said his name is Zach."

"Do you think she's telling the truth?" Uncle Cyrus asked.

I settled more deeply into the booth, my thigh pressed companionably up against Stefon's, and took a sip of wine. Delicious, crisp and light with a slight taste of melons. There was no danger of me becoming a wine snob. But I know what I like and what I liked was this.

"Seems like it, unless she's more skilled than I am and is burying information. But before I could question her more, I realized I was late to dinner. How about you? Did you figure anything else out?"

My uncle shook his head. "I popped into a meeting with some other warlocks and witches in Portland, and none of them have a clue about the book, or what it portends. Our best cryptographers are working on it now."

Even though it made sense, I felt uneasy at the thought that the book was so far away. There was a reason it had shown up in my dreams, then in my shop. And a reason that the key to the book ended up in a dead rat's mouth.

"The key came from the cemetery!" I blurted out, jerking my hand and crashing into Stefon's hand just as he was about to take another sip of beer.

Cyrus looked around the restaurant, body tense. I must've been kind of loud.

Oops.

Luckily, the place was only half full, and no one seemed to have noticed my little outburst.

Stefon mopped up some spilled beer with his napkin, as a waiter scurried over with a fresh napkin and a damp cloth.

Once the table was cleaned up, Cyrus leveled me with one of his *You'd better start talking* looks. He'd been giving me those looks since my childhood. You'd think I'd be immune by now, but no. That look still made me want to spill my guts.

Which is a disgusting turn of phrase, when you think about it.

"Babe, you gonna enlighten us, here?" Stefon asked.

"Right. Sorry. If the key was in a dead rat's mouth, it must have come from the cemetery. Did the ghouls have it? But they didn't seem to know anything about a book, and why would they? Was that why Serafina was there that first day? Because the key and book are connected to the centaurs somehow?"

Not that the centaurs would admit to a darn thing if it didn't suit their plans.

"Or did a person plant the key in the rat's mouth after the fact to try and confuse us?" Uncle Cyrus was always the voice of reason, but his words just didn't ring true. I think he knew it, too.

"Why would someone plant a key to a witch's book,

though?" he continued thinking aloud. "Only witches and warlocks use the Theban alphabet. And why did the book end up at the shop? It could've been months before you got around to those boxes, right?"

I nodded, taking a slow swallow of my wine. My stomach growled. I really wanted that burger, but there was no waiter in sight.

"Yeah. If it was high season, the box would have stayed in the storeroom until we had a break. But its slow now, so..." I shrugged by way of finishing the sentence.

"Do you think someone knew that?" Stefon asked.

"You mean, the book was planted there?" Cyrus said.

I sat back in the booth and looked out at the choppy gray ocean, suddenly missing my mom. Usually, I thought of Dad because I'd lived with him a lot longer. But Mom? Sometimes I needed her advice, and this was one of those times.

Your parents have been trying to get your attention. But I'd thought that was just the season. Because the veils between the worlds are thinner in October and May. But then there was the dream about the book and the key. Had my mother planted the book?

But how? And how long ago?

The waiter crossed the dining hall, laden with what I hoped were our plates.

"Sarah! Cyrus!" Ash's voice cut across the large space, and I watched the thirteen-year-old racing through the tables, about to intersect with the waiter.

"Ash! Careful!" Jerry called out. Ash's father looked harried, but Ash came to a stop, sneakers squeaking on the hardwood floors.

Father and son approached our table at a more

measured pace, and the waiter followed, looking relieved to have not dumped our dinner on the restaurant floor.

"What are you doing here?" I asked. Costas was too expensive for Jerry and Ash. I knew that because the place was also too expensive for the likes of me. I would never eat here were it not for Cyrus or Stefon, who both made boatloads more money than I did.

Jerry waited to answer until the waiter had set our plates down, as Ash shifted from foot to foot, looking ready to burst.

"Would you like to sit?" Cyrus asked, always gracious.

"We can't stay," Jerry said. "We just needed to let you know that Ash found something out about the book."

"What?" My voice rose, almost to a shriek. This time, other people noticed.

"I didn't crack the whole thing," the teen said, "but I got some of it!"

"How did you even...?" I began, but Cyrus gestured me to silence.

"We should not discuss direct findings in a public place. It's all right to discuss generalities, but not hard information," he said.

"Don't you warlocks have a Cone of Silence or something?" Stefon asked.

"This isn't *Get Smart*, you goof," I shoved my boyfriend playfully. Classic sixties television was another of his geeky hobbies. He smiled but looked slightly abashed.

Cyrus put his cloth napkin on the table and waved a hand for the waiter.

"We're not eating?"

I looked at my hamburger longingly. And the fries

smelled like my idea of heaven, or nirvana, or the Summerlands, or whatever place smells like greasy, salty bliss.

"Much as I dislike the practice, I believe we should take our food to go." Cyrus looked at Jerry and Ash. "May I buy you two dinner as well, in exchange for the information you are about to impart?"

"Yes!" Ash fist pumped the air.

"Ash," Jerry said, looking a bit embarrassed.

"It will save us time, and is the least I can do," Cyrus insisted.

"All right then," Mr. Hamamoto said. His pride was outgunned by an excitable teenager and an implacable warlock. "Two hamburgers to go."

I ate a couple of French fries, because they're best piping hot, and then resigned myself to delayed gratification.

"Soon," I promised the hamburger. "Soon."

26

I'd never actually been all the way inside Ash and Jerry's home. The little cottage was larger than it looked from the outside.

At the front was Jerry's reading room, where he saw clients, then a narrow shoe cupboard and hallway WC tucked beneath a stairway.

After we took off our shoes, Ash had led us to the back of the cottage, which had been opened up to form a large, combination kitchen, dining room, and cozy sitting room, all looking out onto a tidy back garden the size of a handkerchief.

I assumed the bedrooms were upstairs.

"I really like your place," I said, looking around. Blue glazed tiles complemented the slate-gray kitchen cupboards, and there was a jewel-green sofa and a comfy looking, battered leather chair in the sitting room.

Stefon, Cyrus, and I sat at a round wood dining table that properly fit four. Luckily, Ash was tiny, and his dad was very thin, so we'd been able to squeeze around once

Ash and Jerry finished bustling about, getting cutlery and glasses for the pitcher of water in the center of the table.

"Thanks," said Jerry, passing the cutlery around and pulling out a chair. "We like it."

We all tucked into our food, which I was thankful for. No way was I going to be able to concentrate on Theban cyphers and keys in dead rats' mouths unless I ate something.

The burger was delicious. I saw why Stefon ordered them all the time. The fries were barely warm, but still crunched between my teeth, so I was happy enough.

Once half the food was gone, Cyrus cleared his throat and wiped his mouth with a paper towel Ash had given us all to use as napkins.

"So, Ash, what have you uncovered?"

The boy's narrow face lit up. He swiped at his fingers and face with his own paper towel, then shoved back from the table.

"Be right back!" he said, racing off down the hallway in his stockinged feet.

Ash returned with a tablet and a notebook, a pen held between his teeth. We cleared some space at the table for him. His eyes danced with excitement. There's nothing better than a curious kid who's found something. That warmed my little nerdy heart.

"So," he said. "I took pictures of some of the pages just to see if I could help out Tracy and Tabitha, you know? I like puzzles, and this felt like a puzzle."

"Plus, he's been studying Bletchley Park recently," his dad said indulgently, as if a thirteen-year-old studying World War II codebreakers was a cute quirk, like loving Minecraft or unicorns.

"I'm impressed, Ash," Stefon said. And I could tell he was.

Ash looked pleased at the comment. I think he had a little bit of hero worship happening with Stefon. I made a note to ask my boyfriend if he would ever include Ash in one of his D&D campaigns.

Ash had made a few friends here in Seashell Cove, but the bullying he'd gotten for being a geeky trans boy in the town he and Jerry had fled had clearly left a mark. A little more nurturing from various quarters would only do Ash good.

"So," Ash said, flipping open his notebook and rifling through some pages, "I wasn't able to get like whole paragraphs, but I think I found some words. I was studying the Theban alphabet. Like you said, Sarah, a few of the words seem to make words in English. But these here?"

He pointed to various random words in his notebook. We all leaned across the table to look.

"I think part of the code is they must be in a different language."

"Like German or French or Spanish?" I asked, waving a French fry in the air.

"Yeah, but I don't know enough about those languages, except a little bit of Spanish, so I'm not really sure."

"Show us what you got," Stefon said, leaning over.

I didn't often get to see this side of my boyfriend. I mean, of course, I knew it was there. He's a major geek and doesn't hide it. But usually he indulges in these kinds of activities with his friends, not around mine. It stood to reason that ciphers would be his jam.

"Well, see, these letters here repeat. And then there's a

change and I started to see the pattern of the words and interspersed with whatever other language that is? That's the thing I figured out," he said, looking around the table to make sure we were following.

We all just nodded and motioned for him to continue. Cyrus looked particularly intent.

"So, if I read between the words, just the English ones, or at least the ones that seem to make sense as English, here's what I found."

He cleared his throat and started reciting.

"The one who was born between light and dark, and earth and air. The one who travels near and far, and here and there. The one who lives betwixt and between, who is more than what at first, it seems... They will hold the power."

Ash sat back in his chair and took a big gulp of water.

"Well," Stefon said, "that's intense."

"Yeah, isn't it cool? What do you think it means, Sarah?"

I looked from Ash's expectant eyes toward my uncle. Cyrus shook his head, but was stroking his chin, deep in thought.

Okay. Up to me, then. I closed my eyes and took a breath.

"Ash, can you read that one more time?"

He did. I kept my eyes closed and my breathing even, letting the words wash over me. And then I got it.

"We've been looking at this all wrong." My eyes snapped open. "We were thinking it was either a faery or a human and something else. Or maybe a changeling. But what I think..."

"Just say it, Sarah." Uncle Cyrus's voice held that *Stop waffling* tone.

"I think it's not a changeling. I think it's not two beings. I think it's one being."

Everyone looked confused.

How to explain?

"I think it's someone who was born from a faery parent and a human parent. I think we have a being here that is both."

"Is that even possible?" Jerry furrowed his brow.

"I've heard of such things," Cyrus said, "but never encountered one. But Sarah, I think you're right. I think we're looking for a human–faery mix."

"And I think I know who it is," I replied.

"Who?" everyone said.

I turned to Jerry's son. "Ash?"

"Yeah. I didn't want to say unless someone else said first, because I wasn't sure, but yeah, I think it's the kid from the trailer park."

"Zach. Tessa thinks his name is Zach. If it's the same kid, that is."

But of course it was the same kid. It had to be. My mind grasped at all of the possibilities, flipping through all of our suspects: The kid. The strange man. Roddy Devall. Tessa...

I didn't want to confront Zach, not yet. We'd already frightened him off, and I didn't want to risk him running if we went on another fishing expedition. We needed to rule out some other people, first. Maybe get some more information to approach him with.

Tessa might have more answers, but I wasn't sure exactly where her trailer was parked.

"We need to talk to Roddy Devall."

"What does the town realty agent have to do with any of this?" Jerry asked.

"Heck if I know," I replied. "But he's up to something, and I aim to find out what. Besides, he's hanging around with a new man who seems off to me."

And someone had blinded Máni and Tessa, hadn't they? Surely the kid wasn't powerful enough to do that?

"Off how?" Stefon asked.

"He might be fae, but I can't quite tell."

"And you think Roddy and this man are involved because...?"

I shrugged, because I didn't have a good answer, just another hunch. And sometimes all a witch and a Justice has to rely upon is instinct and intuition.

And when clues are thin on the ground, almost anyone can become a suspect, can't they?

27

Everyone knew where Roddy Devall lived. He made sure of it.

He had the fanciest house at the top of the hill. The one with the best view. The one that an old Seashell Cove family had moved out of in shame after the bank had foreclosed.

A Realtor needs the best place in town, he bragged when he bought the place. He then set about fixing it up, though what had needed fixing, I couldn't tell.

It was the kind of house—a large, two-story beauty, with large windows and a gorgeous old walnut door— that anyone but the most moneyed and vain would be proud to call home.

Stefon pulled into the long driveway, with me and Cyrus the only other passengers. Jerry didn't want Ash to be part of the confrontation, so those two had wisely stayed at home.

As soon as Stefon stopped the car, I unbuckled myself from the back seat and barreled out, racing up to the front porch. My boots smacked on the broad wood planks as I rushed toward the gleaming, polished door. Grabbing the brass knocker, I pounded with all my might.

No response. Which was a little anticlimactic. I guess it felt like Roddy should've been waiting for us. But then, I have a tendency to build up confrontations in my mind, and had been going over things in my head the whole drive.

The porch boards creaked as Stefon and Cyrus stepped up behind me.

"Anyone home, babe?"

"If he is, he's not answering."

I pounded on the door again and then rang the bell three times for good measure. Finally, I heard footsteps inside.

Roddy opened the door, looking slightly less put together than usual. There were even a few hairs out of place.

"Sarah Braxton?" His face screwed up in confusion.

"Yes, and I'm here to talk to you."

"I don't understand.... I have company. I'm a little bit busy."

"I bet you are," I growled.

"Babe." Stefon put a hand on my shoulder. I shrugged it off.

"I bet I know exactly who's here. It's a well-dressed man with pale hair and pockets full of cash to buy houses with, isn't it?"

Roddy's face flushed red. "It's none of your business who I may have here."

"It's all right, Roddy." A mellifluous voice came from behind him. "Let them in and ask what they want."

"I will do no such thing," said Roddy. The preternaturally beautiful man stepped up behind him in his stocking feet. He was tall and slender. I would have said he was delicate because his wrists and neck were so finely boned, but delicate was the last word I could use to describe this man.

Although whatever strange, fae quality I had sensed in Angie's café was gone. Standing before me was just an ordinary man.

"I don't believe we've been introduced," he said with a slight smile. Huh. He actually seemed genuine. "My name is Callum. And you're Sarah, I believe?"

"Yes. Pleased to meet you," I said grudgingly. Manners forced me to hold out my hand. We shook. His fingers were thin, and cool to the touch.

"We were just having a drink," he said. "Roddy was kind enough to invite me here because I don't yet know anyone in town."

"She's not coming in," Roddy said. "Sarah, what do you want?"

"Have there been any dead rats on your porch lately, Roddy?"

His eyes grew wide. "I...I..." he stammered. "What do you mean? Dead rats? Why would there be dead rats?"

Sweat popped up on his forehead despite the chill October air.

"Well, several of us have received some little presents on our shop stoops lately. You mean to tell me you haven't?"

"No," he said, shaking his head. Was that genuine confusion? Or was he bluffing? "I have no idea what you're talking about. Do I need to?"

"You should know," Stefon said. "That's why we came. To make sure you were aware that this was happening."

Good save, Stefon.

"It sounds more as if *she* was accusing me of leaving the rats. Isn't that right Sarah?"

Or not. I deflated. All my anger and fear left and standing before me was an ordinary man.

A greedy, loathsome man, to be sure. And behind him was just another man. Handsome, yes, but not a magical creature after all.

Gah. I hate being wrong.

"I'm sorry to take up your time. I'm just scared and upset and looking for answers."

"That's understandable," said Callum. "I would be scared, too, as a matter of fact. I wonder if I should rethink buying a place here. This seemed like such a quiet, sleepy town. That was part of the attraction."

Callum looked up, as if pondering leaving.

Roddy blanched, likely envisioning piles of money floating away.

"I assure you, nothing like this ever happens here!" he said. "Seashell Cove is a nice, sleepy town. Well, we get a little busy during tourist season, but you won't mind that. Would you?"

Roddy sounded almost desperate for Callum to agree.

Callum patted Roddy's arm. "We'll see. I won't give up on this town yet."

"Callum, where did you say you came from?" Cyrus asked.

Something flickered across the man's eyes. But then his face brightened as his green eyes took in my handsome, dapper uncle. Actually, they were quite a matched set in a way. Roddy bristled at the attention being paid to my uncle, but he got it under control pretty quickly.

"I didn't say," Callum said. "I come from back east and wanted a quieter life. I needed a change."

Cyrus nodded. "Well, I think we've taken up enough of your time. So sorry to disturb."

"All right," Roddy said. "See you around, I guess."

After he shut the door, I whirled on Cyrus.

"What the heck was that about?" I whispered.

"I'm not sure," Cyrus murmured, as we stepped off the porch. "But you're right. Something's off about those two. I was trying to read them."

"And?" I asked. We walked back to Stefon's SUV.

Cyrus just shook his head.

After we were all buckled up, Stefon spoke.

"What does it mean? That you got nothing? I didn't either, though I could have sworn that guy seemed fae before."

"It means," Cyrus said, "that either they are both completely innocent, ordinary human beings, or someone named Callum is very, very good at cloaking."

28

There was nothing for it. We were going to have to confront the kid, and much as I hated it, we needed Ash's help. No way would the kid let us get close enough without another kid around.

A kid he maybe even trusted.

So here we were, back in The Kelpie's dining room because it was the only place large enough to hold everyone, especially since the centaurs wanted to attend.

Unfortunately, so did the lead ghoul. And since one of their own had been murdered, I didn't feel like we could cut them off.

Even creatures I disliked had rights. That was how being Justice worked.

Liam and Sophie were polite about the ghouls, but all the doors and windows were open to let out the microwaved-fish-and-graveyard stench.

Tabitha's parents both showed up, too. I couldn't tell if Tabitha was pleased or embarrassed by this, but I guess that was the typical response of any teenager, whether or not their parents were vampires.

Rhiannon had insisted on attending, which she was doing more and more often, and sat on the table between Stefon and I. Preston sat next to her, scratching her head.

::I'm tired of being left out of the action,:: Rhiannon said through her purrs. *::Besides, I'm the one with the best ideas.::*

I was not about to argue with her. Especially not when she started flexing her razor paws in bliss.

Carol and Tracy hurried in through the bar, followed by Patricia. She was moving slowly, but looked much better than last time I saw her, which considering she'd bee knocked out at the time, wasn't saying much.

Stefon leapt to his feet and guided the pottery teacher to a chair next to mine. My knight in geeky armor. I patted his arm in thanks after he sat back down.

"What's that smell?" Tracy blurted, clapping a hand over her mouth and blushing furiously when she saw the ghoul. "I-I'm sorry!"

The ghoul scowled, but didn't say anything, so I figured all was good. Or as good as it was going to get from an entity that had really looked as if it was going to kill me in the cemetery. Being surrounded by ghouls isn't something I want to experience again.

I turned to the two centaurs who were crowding the doorway that led into the courtyard. Máni looked much better, I was glad to see. Hopefully, he was clear-headed enough that we could get more information out of him tonight than the last time I'd seen him.

::Are you starting this meeting or what?:: Bunny asked. She tapped the toe of her T-strap shoe impatiently, which

set the beaded fringe on her gown to shimmering and shaking.

I cleared my throat, and then fought down a gag.

"I'm sorry," I said, turning to the ghoul. "Can you stand in the courtyard near an open window and still hear okay?"

"Of all the disss-respectful..."

"Stop it!" Serafina barked out. The ghoul looked as if he'd been smacked in his decaying face, but ducked his head and complied, shoving out the door past the two centaurs. Serafina snapped her teeth at him as he went, a sight which terrified me, but barely affected the ghoul at all.

When the ghoul was in place near the window, I clapped my hands.

"All right. Let's start this thing. First of all, I'll begin with what we think we know. We now know the ghouls could not have planted the rats, but that the rats were stolen from the ghouls at the cemetery. Is that correct?"

"It issss," the ghoul's voice filtered through the window.

"Okay, on our current suspect list is still Tessa. I don't believe it's her, although she seems to be hiding something and I don't know what." I held up another finger, counting off. "Then there's Roddy Devall, who I really dislike and want to be the culprit. But I'm not so sure about him, either. And then there's the man he was with. Callum."

"Callum? Who's that?" Sophie asked.

"He's new in town," I said. "Some high roller Roddy has been helping with real estate."

Who seemed fae the first couple of times I saw him, but then didn't when I was close up and personal.

"And helping Roddy with some other estate," Stefon muttered. I poked him to make him be quiet.

"Cyrus thinks there might be something suspicious about him. But again, no proof. And that brings us to the kid from the trailer park. Stefon and I tried to talk to him the other day, but he raced off into the woods."

"Why is he a suspect?" Tabitha's mother asked.

I looked at the vampire. If you didn't know Lisa was undead, you might think was just a very attractive, young-looking, albeit pale, Asian woman.

"Do you want to tell them, Ash?"

He nodded gravely, and opened up his notebook on the table.

"Things have been confused because we weren't sure if we were dealing with a human or a faery, or some something else. And we weren't sure if it was three people, or two or one."

"And we still don't know that for certain," Uncle Cyrus interjected.

Ash nodded. "Right. Don't make assumptions. That's what you always say, right, Dad?"

Jerry nodded his head, looking proud of his son. "Go on, Ash."

"But then there was the book that Tracy and Tabitha and Cyrus were working on translating. And I took some pictures of it and brought it home because I like puzzles, you know, ciphers."

We all nodded.

"Tell us what you found," Cyrus said, keeping his voice gentle.

"Well, it's a mix of languages, like, interspersed. But the English parts I could make out talked about a person who was neither one thing or another. And so I talked to Sarah and Cyrus about it, and we seem to think the book might be talking about someone who's half faery and half human."

"A changeling?" Serafina's voice was sharp.

"Not a changeling," I said. "Someone with one parent who's human and one parent from the faery realms."

"Huh," Serafina said, crossing her arms over her chest.

"I could see how that makes sense." Máni looked at me. "Except the magic that took me out was definitely fae. I don't see any way that someone even half human could wield that amount of power. I was deflated."

::And would the child have murdered a ghoul?:: Rhiannon asked. ::And why?::

Dang. More good questions. I was so sure we'd had the answer in this kid.

"Well," I said, "maybe we're back to square one. But in any case, we still need a plan to go talk to this kid. And we're going to need your help, Ash."

I looked at Ash, but then I looked at his father, who nodded.

"Ash and I discussed it," he said, putting his hand on the young man's shoulder, "and he has a protective amulet to wear. And with enough of us around, I'm hoping we can keep him safe."

"We'll definitely keep him safe," Ah Lam Wu said. "Cyrus and I can make a protective bubble around him."

"But..." Ash looked nervous all of a sudden.

"But what, Ash?" I asked.

"But if he's half faery, won't he be able to tell that I've got magic around me?"

Dang, yet another good point.

"Ordinarily, yes," Ah Lam said, "but we can devise it so that an ordinary scan won't show it."

"That's right," Cyrus said. "Someone would have to be very determined to read you for it to show up at all."

Which made me think of Callum, except Cyrus *had* probed his energy fields.

I threw up my hands.

"What was that for?" Delta asked, sounding grumpy.

"I can't catch hold of the threads of this case. I keep feeling as if there's something very important, just off to one side."

"Be that as it may," Uncle Cyrus said, "we need to decide what to do. Who's going to go talk to the kid and who's going to prepare for whatever comes next?"

"We centaurs can surround the area, blocking off egress into the woods," Serafina said.

Well, that was good.

"And we can bring a host of ghoulssss to frighten anyone who gets passsst the centaurs."

"Thank you," I said.

"And we'll talk to the kid," Ash said. "You're right, by the way. His name is Zach. Patricia told Carol. But where will you be, Sarah?"

"Stefon and I will be just around the corner," I replied.

"And I can fit you up with a comms device," Stefon said.

"Like spies?" Ash asked, eyes lighting up.

"Just like that. You'll have an earpiece and a wire that

are practically invisible. That will alert us if anything goes wrong."

Jerry took Ash's hands. "For that to work, you'll need a word or phrase to use that will sound ordinary in conversation, but will tell us if you need help. Can you think of anything?"

Ash screwed up his face for a moment. Then nodded.

"Yeah, I'll say I really wish I had some butterscotch ice cream."

I grinned. "That's perfect."

"When do we get ice cream?" Preston asked.

::*Yeah, when do we get ice cream?*:: Rhiannon echoed.

I shushed the two miscreants.

"I like butterscotch too, kid," Stefon said, smiling.

"Oh, I don't like butterscotch at all," Ash replied, face serious. "That's how you'll know I'm in trouble."

We all laughed at that. It felt really good. I wished I didn't have the feeling that it would be the last laugh we shared together for a while.

29

It was Sunday afternoon in the shop, and I had ants in my pants.

Tracy and Tabitha were continuing with their Halloween decorating as Carol sat in the chair one of the chairs beneath the stained glass window in the middle of the store. Biff was floating around somewhere. He'd been throwing books all morning, until I finally shouted at him to knock it off.

It was the first time I'd ever shouted at him, and now Biff was sulking. It wasn't the best situation, but what can I say? I was a little tense.

There were exactly zero customers in the store to take my mind off what we had planned. I hadn't decided whether that was good or bad.

Stefon, Cyrus, and Ah Lam were set to meet us here around closing time, so we could make final plans before heading down to the trailer park, to check in with the kid whose name turned out was Zach.

Patricia had finally recovered enough to tell Carol

about him. She'd gone to the casino to visit his mom, who worked two jobs, and to see if Zach needed anything. I guess he did his homework in the casino on the nights his mom had to work there.

He was one of Patricia's pottery students. But she'd never noticed anything off about him, other than the usual issues a poor kid had.

She'd also agreed to meet Máni at the edge of the parking lot after seeing the kid's mom. They were courting, I guess. Or friends. And that's when the flash and the weird occurrences happened.

The bells at the front door shook and clattered. Rhiannon and I both looked up. Me, from the accounting program on the computer, and Rhiannon from where she was dozing on the end of the counter.

Speaking of, it was Patricia herself, blond hair tucked beneath a knitted burgundy cap that matched her burgundy raincoat. Her face was pinched with worry.

"Hey," Patricia said.

"Are you okay?" I asked.

She shook her head as she approached the counter.

"I'm really worried about Zach." She leaned against the counter opposite me. "His mom said the dad has been hanging around lately. Making trouble."

I sighed. Battles between parents were always hard. Maybe that's why Zach had been acting up. And he was the one Tessa was trying to protect. Did Tessa know about Zach's dad, too?

I wished we'd had this information before. We could have ruled Zach out.... It now seemed as if he wasn't our half-fae, half-human creature, but an ordinary boy, caught between two adults.

Which meant there just might be two kids. And that meant I was back at square one. I stifled a sigh.

"Can I get you a cup of tea?" I asked.

She shook her head again. "No, I'm too wired already."

"I get that," I replied.

"You're sure you won't get hurt? That anyone won't get hurt? Zach is so vulnerable…"

"Frankly, at this point, we may call the whole thing off. But if we don't, we're going to do our best to make sure both Zach and Ash are well protected, but I can't actually make any promises. You know that right?"

She nodded.

"Carol's sitting back under the stained glass if you want to join her."

Patricia nodded again and wandered back, tracing her fingertips along the bookcases as she went.

I hated this part of my job. It had to be hard to try to be a mentor to a kid you thought was in danger, and who was either in danger from the same thing that zapped Patricia and laid her out on the parking lot tarmac, or from an ordinary father, making trouble.

But did that mean we should stick with our plan, or not? The clock was ticking, and as Justice, I needed to decide.

I saw movement out the front windows and looked.

::*Holy moly. Is that who I think it is?*:: Rhiannon asked.

"Tracy? Tabitha?" I called softly. "I think Zach is here. Text Ash and Jerry?"

Guess we didn't have until tonight to prepare. And guess the plan was proceeding, whether I wanted it to or not.

"On it," Tabitha replied.

"And I'll text Cyrus," Tracy said. Tracy had Cyrus's phone number? That was news to me. I could barely get my uncle to answer my own texts.

"Good morning."

The bells clanged again, and the young man who'd run from me at the trailer park stepped in, followed by a woman in her mid-thirties. She had short dark hair and dark circles under her eyes. She looked exhausted.

"Welcome to The Widening Gyre," I said.

"Thanks," she said. "Do you have any used kids' books? The library is closed and this one here has read everything at home."

"Sure do. Down the side aisle, halfway back." I pointed. "Let me know if you need any help."

::What are you going to do?:: Rhiannon asked.

::I'm not sure,:: I thought back. *::Can you go keep an eye on them?::*

::Sure thing. I'll tell Posey and Petal to do the same.::

"Already on it," a gravelly gargoyle voice said.

Rhiannon padded her way through the bookshelves, and I heard a boy's voice saying, "Oh look, a kitty. Can I pet you?"

Of course, you can pet her. Rhiannon is a glutton for scritches.

I tapped my fingers on the countertop. *Come on, Cyrus you can show up any time now.*

Then, for good measure, I texted Liam and Tetris as well, and Delta too, sending out a blast alert group text.

En route, Stefon replied. *Hang tight.*

As I read those words, I gave a little sigh of relief.

Then the bells clanged again and in walked Cyrus and Ah Lam Wu.

"Thank Hecate you're here," I murmured.

They both nodded.

"Where are they?" Ah Lam whispered.

"Kids' books," I said. So much for our careful plan with ghouls, and centaurs, and everything else.

"Should I talk to him?" I asked. "Patricia just told me his dad has been hanging around, causing trouble. He might not be our changeling or whatever. We need more info!"

Cyrus shook his bald head. "Give it a moment."

Great. Just what I was good at: waiting around for something to happen.

I looked from Cyrus to Angelica. "Do to have any way to contact the centaurs or the ghouls?"

"I can do that," she said, rushing back out the door.

Not that it would do any good, I thought. They couldn't come this close to town. Besides, it was daylight. We weren't supposed to do this until full dark, which wasn't for another hour and a half.

I saw Roddy Devall scurry by and across the street. And Tetris was talking to Tessa. What the heck was going on? Why was everyone around right? It was almost as if someone or something had planned this confrontation.

But why now? And why here on my turf?

"I have to go see what he's doing," I said to Cyrus.

He followed me down the aisle. Zach was busy leafing through books as his mother leaned against a bookcase, eyes closed. She looked like she needed a long hot bath. But more likely, she needed a better paying job and childcare.

I saw now why Patricia did her best by all the kids in town. Speaking of which... I quickly changed direction and headed down the far aisle along the side wall bearing down on the reading nook beneath the stained glass that showed a pile of books. Carol and Patricia were sitting there. They both looked up.

"Zach and his mother are here," I said quietly.

"I'll go talk to them," Patricia said.

I jerked my head toward the next aisle over and the pottery teacher hurried away. I heard her greeting the second the phone in my pocket buzzed.

Stefon. *Just outside heading in with Delta and Tetris.*

The bells clanged, and I headed back to the front counter to greet my friends, but pulled up short.

It decidedly not my friends standing in front of me, but a handsome, dapper man with pale hair and nice shoes.

But this time he didn't look like a nice man at all. This time, green eyes glowed, and power practically snapped from his long, pale, fingertips.

"Hello, Sarah Braxton. We meet again."

30

"**Y**ou're fae!" I blurted. Smooth, Sarah.

The handsome man smirked. "Took you long enough to figure that out."

Rhiannon stood on the counter and hissed.

"You cloak yourself well," Cyrus said. He approached the counter in a stately fashion, as if there was nothing more on his mind than looking fabulous and powerful. Carol and Patricia stood practically shoulder to shoulder at the end of one of the central aisles. I could tell they were trying to block something.

I assumed that something was Zach and his mother. Whispers came from the back of the shop. The teens. A crunch of stone from above told me that both gargoyles were on watch.

We still had some wild cards, too. Angelica, Stefon, Delta, and Tetris were just outside somewhere. I hoped Tabitha and Tracy were texting information out.

All of a sudden, I missed Cecilia. She should be back in town by now, but was probably nestled in with Toby, her partner. The non-binary hob liked nothing more than being at home, and my best friend seemed content to oblige.

But still, I could use some of her bravado right about now.

Inhaling, I channeled my best short-Asian-bisexual-fuchsia-haired-badass-mechanic self. Which given my height, breadth, and sheer whiteness, isn't easy. At least I had the bisexual part going for me.

::*And you're a witch. And Justice.*:: Rhiannon reminded me.

Oh yeah. All of that. Something about this guy really messed with my head.

"Why are you here?" I asked.

"I think you know," the fae man replied. He raised his head and pitched his voice toward the back of the shop. "I'm here for my son."

Rhiannon growled. I almost growled myself. Instead, I stepped closer to the faery man, and looked into those flashing green eyes.

"I don't know who you are, or who you think you are, but if your son wanted to be with you, don't you think he already would be?"

I knew my words were not one hundred percent true but didn't care. I just wanted to rattle his cage a bit. See how deep the tiger was hiding.

He raised the side of his lip, as if he wanted to snarl, but caught himself, and wiped the expression from his face in an instant.

Score one for the witch.

"If there is some sort of custodial dispute," Cyrus said, "I am certain the Council will be happy to be of assistance."

My uncle leaned against the counter, cool as can be. His words were also pointed. There was no way this was a clear custodial issue. Not when mother and child had been living in near poverty in a trailer park on the edge of town. Not when Daddy-o here was dressed in cashmere.

"Zachary Linden, I can smell you. I know you are here. You as well, Patricia."

For the first time in my life, I really wished the book-shop had a back exit. As it was, I hoped the teens and Biff had found a way to hide the boy.

The bells to the shop clanged, and in sauntered Stefon, his bulk filling the entryway. He was followed by Tetris and Delta, and I could see Preston's purple cap peeking from Delta's tote bag.

"Hey babe." Stefon walked up to me and kissed my temple. "What's going on?"

He smiled at the fae man, and held out his hand.

"I'm Stefon."

Fae man was startled, and took it, eyes widening slightly as Stefon's huge, dark hand engulfed his more delicate pale one. Then his green eyes flashed a warning. Stefon yelped and jerked his hand back.

I wrinkled my nose against the scent of singed hair.

The fae man smirked.

"You'll not get my name that easily, human."

"Just being polite, man," Stefon said, as the exhausted-looking woman stepped out from between Carol and Patricia.

"Callum," she said, voice weary and resigned. "What are you doing here?"

He moved like a cat toward the woman. "Brigid. Not

as beautiful as you once were. Tsk. Tsk. Tsk. You've really let yourself go, haven't you?"

Her tired brown eyes flashed with anger. "You work in a restaurant all day, and a casino at night, and care for a growing child's needs, and run a household on a pittance, and we'll see how nice and shiny you look."

He raised his hands and shook his head, smiling, as if his words and presence were pure innocence.

I was tempted to sic Rhiannon on him.

Cyrus gestured to me. I raised an eyebrow in question. He jerked his gleaming bald head toward the door. I nudged Stefon and did the same.

My boyfriend, bless him, understood immediately and went to block the exit without looking like he was blocking the exit. Being six-foot-three and umpteen pounds of flesh and muscle makes that easy.

"Where is the boy, Brigid?"

"You'll never touch him again."

He laughed. It sounded like nails on a chalkboard and breaking glass. I shuddered.

"I would have had him already, if it weren't for that odious *potter* and her pet centaur."

The potter, Patricia, straightened her spine and stepped to Brigid's side. "Zach is a good boy. You don't deserve him. He asked for my help because he is afraid of you."

It was all clear to me now. This creature had blasted Patricia and Máni.

We'd known the father was threatening Zach. We just hadn't known the father was fae.

::Now that you know, what are we going to do about it?::

I glared at Rhiannon, who stared back with implacable green eyes. She was right, and she knew it.

What was taking Ah Lam Wu so long?

We had planned any confrontation for outdoors. I didn't want my bookshop trashed by a magical battle.

::Sarah....:: With a rush of cold, Biff was at my side. *::Your parents want you to fight. Your father says to heck with the store, and I do, too. This child is special. His life is worth more than any books.::*

I felt a pang that my parents could communicate so clearly with Biff, and not with me. But at least a clear message had finally come through. I also wanted to argue with Biff and my dad, but couldn't. Of course, a human's life was worth more than all the stories held within these four walls. Books could be replaced. Zach could not.

Inhaling deeply, I squared my shoulders, planted my black boots on the floor, and hitched up my jeans. I could channel Cecilia, and Stefon, and Cyrus. I could channel all my friends.

But mostly, I could channel who I was: Sarah Endora Braxton, child of two powerful witches, book nerd, and Justice of Seashell Cove.

"Callum," I said. "If you want Zach, you're going to have to get through me."

It felt as if everything in the shop took a collective breath. I felt my friends square off around me.

Tracy and Tabitha stepped forward from the stacks.

"You're going to have to get through all of us," Tabitha said.

My heart filled with gratitude and pride.

::Let's kick some faery butt,:: Rhiannon said.

"You don't know what you are saying, witch." Callum glowered.

"I know exactly what I'm saying, faery man. I am a witch who knows that words have power. And what I want to say to you is…"

Callum slowly raised his hand.

"Sarah!" a gravelly voice squeaked from above. It was Posey. "Duck!"

31

I ducked just as a large rock with wings hurtled past my head, knocking into Callum's shoulder. The elf shot he'd been about to cast at my heart went wild, shooting through the latest Harlan Coben on the front counter display.

Everything went wild. There was shouting, and flailing, and a roaring in my ears.

Center, Sarah. Feel your power. That was my mother's voice. The thing I always thought of as my own inner wisdom? It was her. I blinked away tears, and did as she said, trusting my friends to do what they each did best, as I found my center point and inhaled, calling forth my magic.

Magic rose through me, flowing up from the earth beneath the building and into my feet. It flowed toward me from all the stories, every book, every photograph, and piece of art in the bookshop. I felt Biff, Petal, Posey, Rhiannon. I felt Uncle Cyrus, Carol, Preston, Delta Crabbit, and the teens. I felt Stefon. And I felt the bookshop itself.

Everything rallied to my aid. To Zach's aid.

Where was Zach?

As soon as the thought left my head, it was answered.

"I've got him." That was Petal's voice, coming somewhere from the back of the shop. "He's doing fine."

That thought taken care of, I faced down Callum once again. He was flinging faerie bolts and elf shot left and right, taking out stacks of books and journals, singing paper and bookshelves, and generally making a mess.

Cyrus and Delta kept the worst of it contained, which was good. If I knew my business wasn't about to burn to the ground, I could focus on the task at hand.

Taking out Callum.

"Are you always such a nuisance?" I asked.

His green eyes blazed with anger.

"Roddy was right, you are an uppity woman."

Huh. Good on my instincts for not liking the realty agent.

"I have a right to my boy!" he roared, flinging green faerie fire my way.

I deflected it with a wave of my hand. It felt easy. Too easy. Was he holding back? Or...

::*We're all feeding you our power.::* That was Tracy's voice in my head. ::*The space is too tight for all of us to fight him, so we're giving you all we've got.::*

Could everyone use mind speech now? Clearly, I needed to catch up.

"Carol and I've been teaching both the teens," Cyrus said, as he snuffed out another flame.

"Thanks for letting me know!" I replied, blocking another blow.

"Pay attention!" Callum shouted. "Why aren't you paying attention to me!"

I laughed. "Don't like it when things are about someone other than you, do you? Well, too bad!"

I channeled the group's collective power, weaving a shining net of magic.

He shot a bolt toward my hands. I dodged and ducked, and it flew past me, taking out three of the dangling witch's hats hanging above the counter. So much for the teens' Halloween decorations.

Posey flew around the fae man's head, distracting him. Rhiannon leapt to the floor and began swatting at his ankles and biting his legs.

He danced as if covered in fire ants, trying to shake the gargoyle and the cat.

::*Good job, you two,*:: I thought, as I re-centered myself and continued weaving my magical net.

::*Get ready, everyone!*::

The mayhem continued around me, books toppling, Rhiannon yowling, the gargoyle screaming, and Callum hitting me with blast after blast.

He had somehow found a way to attack me even with all the distractions being flung his way.

I had to get this net around him, and fast.

"Cyrus! Help me contain his magic!"

"This one's on you!" my uncle shouted. "The magic needs a single point!"

Okay. Great. I'd ask about that, later, too.

I drew in more and more power, dodging and

crouching as my mind and hands and will worked to weave the net of containment.

"Zach, no!" Petal screamed on full blast.

I winced. A body hurtled itself into my back, wrapping skinny arms around my waist, giving me a magic push. The net flew from my fingertips and wrapped around Callum's head, then torso, arms, and legs, and feet.

The faery goggled, eyes wide, then froze, hands and legs stiff as a board.

And then he fell to one side.

"Stefon!" I screamed.

My boyfriend caught the faery man right before he hit the ground.

I looked down at the boy wrapped around me.

"Zach?" I asked.

He looked up at me with somber brown eyes wet with tears.

"I couldn't let him get you. I just couldn't."

Then his mother was there, crouched at his side, hugging him and crying.

Stefon walked toward me, through the fallen books and singed displays and wrapped his big arms around me.

I breathed in, smelling his special Stefon scent.

It smelled like home.

32

Pity there was still work to do. I gave Stefon a big squeeze, then we released each other.

Scrubbing at my face, I looked around at all my friends gathered in my crowded little shop.

"Thank you all," I said. Then I turned to my uncle and Ah Lam. She must have arrived after Callum hit the floor and I was otherwise occupied.

"We need to banish him back to Underhill. But I'm not sure how to make sure he stays there. Any ideas?"

Ah Lam tapped one perfectly manicured nail against her lips as Cyrus stroked his chin. As they thought about it, I walked over to Zach and Brigid. The woman looked shell shocked, and the boy looked strangely resigned. Almost as if he knew this was coming.

"Brigid, before I sentence your husband..."

"Ex," she whispered.

"Right. Before I sentence your ex-husband, is there anything you want or need? Any provisions for you and Zach?"

It was clear Callum hadn't exactly been paying child support for his half-faery son. Not if Brigid was working two jobs and living in a trailer park on the edge of town.

She lifted her chin and straightened her spine. "We need money. Enough that I don't have to work so much, and so Zach has everything he needs. And I'd like to fix up the trailer, too. Make some repairs."

That surprised me. "You don't want him to buy you a nice house in town?"

He'd been looking at properties with Roddy, after all. Surely that meant he could spring for a nice place. That is, if the meetings with Roddy hadn't just been a ruse to get closer to Zach and steal him from his mother.

Brigid shook her head and squeezed Zach's shoulders.

"I like the quiet of being just outside town, and Zach likes living with the forest right there, don't you? Especially since that one centaur has been visiting."

Zach nodded.

A half-fae kid wanting to live in the forest made sense, but centaurs visiting? That must be Máni. Was everyone in town trying to help this boy?

Why hadn't anyone told me? It isn't as if I would have reported the boy to the magic authorities or anything.

Ah well.

"Okay," I said. "I'll make sure he pays. Zach? Do you want to say anything to your father before we send him on his way?"

Zach set his mouth in a line, shoved his shoulders back, and, taking a few steps, stood over his father's bound and prone form.

Callum looked at his son with angry, embarrassed green eyes.

"Thank you for giving me magic. But other than that, you're a pretty terrible father."

Then he turned on his heel and walked back to his mother.

Okay then.

"Cyrus?"

"We figured it out."

"Let's get this over with, then."

I breathed in, and called up the power of the Office of Justice. I felt that magic click into my own. I felt the authority of all the people surrounding me. Then I raised my hands, palms hovering in the air above Callum.

"Callum of Underhill, for murdering a ghoul, and for crimes against humans, centaurs, your former wife, and your own child, I sentence you to give to Zach and Brigid half of your wealth, to be paid in human currency into Brigid's accounts on a monthly basis for as long as Brigid and Zach shall live."

Brigid gasped. Half his wealth must be a lot. Good.

Then Cyrus and Ah Lam raised their hands and began drawing symbols in the air. I saw them in my mind's eye: strange glyphs of unlocking and locking, unbinding, and binding. With my right hand, I traced a door in the air, and with my left, I opened it.

A blinding, silvery light poured out on a wash of rose and apple blossom scents and the sound of chiming bells.

A series of silvery magic chains wrapped Callum's wrists and ankles, and then Cyrus and Ah Lam raised their hands, and Callum levitated off the floor.

"These bindings bar you from the human realms

forever. The rest of the magic shall release you as soon as this doorway is closed," I said.

I turned my head toward my uncle and his partner. "Ready? One. Two. Three!"

With a mighty shove, we got him through the doorway. I quickly slammed it shut and barred it with magic.

I felt the boom resonate on the astral planes, and throughout space and time.

It was finished.

And hopefully, that was the end of dead rats on our doorsteps.

Because I'd had about as much of that as one witch could take.

33

We'd made it to Samhain, and The Kelpie was packed. The speakeasy upstairs was filled with ghosts and anyone else who wanted to listen to music or dance the night away. Last I checked, Uncle Cyrus and Ah Lam Wu were up there, cutting a rug, along with Liam and some other corporeal types.

The centaurs were in the garden, so were a shroud of ghouls—Ash had informed me that shroud is the collective down for this class of undead, and bless them for sparing our noses—and the dining room was filled with laughter. Tessa was there, talking with Tetris and Angie. Clarita, Delta, Carol, and Sophie were deep in conversation, and I could hear Tabitha and Tracy laughing somewhere. I'd seen Jerry and Ash earlier, but they must be holed up somewhere, talking with some of the Wiccans in attendance who had wanted to discuss varying forms of divination with our town expert.

I didn't see Patricia anywhere. She must be in the courtyard with Máni. Humans and centaurs? Who knew?

Food filled the long, central table, and three of the booth tables along the edges of the dining room had been set up as altars. People brought candles, photographs, flowers, and other offerings for their dearly departed.

I stood in front of one of those tables, gazing down at my mother's crystal ball, and my father's favorite book, a first edition of some fairy tales with Arthur Rackham drawings. I'd also set out a piece of apple pie. The only thing I had left to do was light a candle.

The slim white taper in a brass holder was waiting.

Matches in hand, I paused in the midst of the hubbub, took a breath, and closed my eyes.

"Mom and Dad, thanks for all the years you gave me. Thank you for the magic. I miss you, and hope you're together again in the Summerlands, or wherever else you ended up. Thanks for helping me when I need it.

I love you."

I lit a match, sulfur tickling my nose as the flame caught. As I touched match to wick, the crystal ball gave off a single chime.

Then I heard my mother's voice. The voice I'd been waiting for since she died.

::*I'm proud of you, Sarah.*:: Her voice chimed in my head. :: *And you are making a very good Justice, and a very good witch.*::

I sniffed and pressed my fingertips to my eyes to catch the tears pooling there.

"Message received, Mom. Blessed be."

I turned back to the party, still a bit watery-eyed. Stefon caught my eye from across the crowded room. He raised his glass and blew me a kiss. Zach and Brigid threaded their way through the throng.

When they reached me, the smaller woman grasped my hands in hers. She looked much better, as if she'd gotten a decent night's sleep and maybe a good dinner or three.

"Thank you so much," she said. "For everything."

I smiled. "My pleasure. Things are going better, then?"

She nodded. "Much better. I quit my job at the casino and have decided to apprentice with Patricia at the pottery in my spare time. She said I can come over when I'm not working at Costas. Zach loves pottery, and it turns out, so do I."

"That's wonderful news! How are you, Zach?"

The boy shrugged. "Good, I guess. Though I'm kind of sad that I won't see Dad ever again. It was kind of nice at first, him coming around, even if I had to keep it a secret. But then he killed that ghoul and was trying to force me to leave Mom without telling her. So, I started to hide."

And Tessa, Máni, and Patricia tried to protect him. I wish I had known.

That reminded me, there was still one part of the puzzle that I didn't understand.

"Zach, do you know anything about the rats?"

He blanched but nodded. "I told Tessa my dad was trying to take me, and that he'd killed that ghoul and was making threats about you. I figured I should try to warn you and your friends."

"You left rats on people's doorsteps, Zach?"

The boy shuffled, looking really uncomfortable. "That was Dad's idea, at first. He wanted to 'shake up the town' he said. He also wanted to distract you, I think. He forced me to take the rats from the cemetery. But it was my idea to leave the warning. I was trying to alert you that something was wrong."

"Well, that part worked, at least. But did you have to write it in blood?"

He grinned. "I didn't. I took the red paint I use to paint my models and magicked it. Guess it worked."

"Oh boy. You are going to be a handful, aren't you?" I said. "How'd you like to train with Tracy and Tabitha? And maybe Ash could join you all, too."

I didn't think Jerry would mind his son getting a little outside training. And it seemed like Zach would need all the friends he could get.

Zach's face lit up, and he looked excitedly from me to his mother, who was also smiling. "Really? I'm gonna go tell them now!"

He raced off, and Brigid squeezed my hand once more before following her half-fae son.

Delta was waving at me now. Must be time for a toast.

I clapped my hands three times to get everyone's attention, then grabbed a cup from the table and ladled out some warm spiced cider, savoring the smell of cinnamon, allspice, and cloves.

"It's almost midnight, and it's time to make a toast to our beloved dead. So, grab a cup or glass!"

Everyone scurried to get refills. The centaurs and ghouls came closer to the windows.

I raised my cup.

"As we gather together on the edge of winter's cold, let us be thankful for friends and family, for magic and the turning of the year. We honor those who have come before us, and raise our glasses to them, and to a better future, still to come!"

"To the beloved dead!" Delta called.

"To the beloved dead!" we all answered.

"And to the future!" Cyrus called. I hadn't seen my honorary uncle come in, and shot him a smile.

"To the future!"

Then Bunny the flapper popped through the ceiling.

::What are you waiting for, folks? Come dance!::

People laughed and streamed out into the garden, heading for the back stairs leading up to the secret speakeasy on the top floor.

All of a sudden, Stefon's warm, solid, bulk was at my side.

"Happy Samhain, babe."

I looked up into his rich, chocolate-brown eyes, his full mouth framed by that soft beard, and kissed him.

"Happy Samhain, Stefon. May we see many more. Together."

WHAT'S NEXT?

In the midst of the Seashell Cove Solstice preparations, an elf appeared out of nowhere. Frightened, and shivering with cold, all the elf can say is "He is coming." The gargoyles are concerned, and so are the ghosts. Can Rhiannon and Sarah figure out how to help the elf, before the mysterious "he" appears?

Find out in Solstice Witch!

AND MORE...

If you enjoyed this book, please consider telling a friend, or leaving a short review at your favorite booksellers. Many thanks!

And visit thorncoyle.com to sign up for a weekly newsletter.

ACKNOWLEDGMENTS

Thank you to Leslie and Jack for reading, to Dayle for editing, and to my chosen family for years of support.

Most of all, thank you to everyone who fell in love with a witch, a cat, and a wacky seaside town.

By Sun

By Dusk

By Dark

By Witch's Mark

The Panther Chronicles (Complete)

To Raise a Clenched Fist to the Sky

To Wrest Our Bodies From the Fire

To Drown This Fury in the Sea

To Stand With Power on This Ground

The Steel Clan Saga

We Seek No Kings

We Heed No Laws

We Ride at Night

Short Story Collections

A Hint of Faery

A Touch of Faery

A Spark of Magic

A Flame for Yuletide

A Hope for Winter

A Time for Magic

A Speculation of Stars

A Speculation of Hope

A Speculation of Time

Risk It All: Queer Stories of Love, Suspense, And Daring

Thresholds: Queer Stories of Love, Suspense, And Daring

Cats and Other Creatures

NON-FICTION

Evolutionary Witchcraft

Kissing the Limitless

Make Magic of Your Life

Sigil Magic for Writers, Artists & Other Creatives

Crafting a Daily Practice

Resistance Matters

ABOUT THE AUTHOR

T. Thorn Coyle worked in many strange and diverse occupations before settling in to write books full time. Buy them a cup of tea and perhaps they'll tell you about it.

Author of the *Seashell Cove Paranormal Mystery* series, *The Steel Clan Saga*, *The Witches of Portland*, and *The Panther Chronicles*, Thorn's multiple non-fiction books include *Sigil Magic for Writers, Artists & Other Creatives*, and *Evolutionary Witchcraft*.

Thorn's work appears in many anthologies, magazines, and collections. They have taught magical practice in nine countries, on four continents, and in twenty-five states.

An interloper to the Pacific Northwest U.S., Thorn stalks city streets and talks to crows, squirrels, and trees.

Connect with Thorn:
www.thorncoyle.com